WAR OF 24TH CENTURY

Special Thanks To Anurag Mishra

VAIBHAV LOGAR | MEHAK CHHURA | ISHA SINHA

WAR OF 24TH CENTURY

BY

VAIBHAV LOGAR | MEHAK CHHURA | ISHA SINHA

Copyright© VAIBHAV LOGAR & MEHAK CHHURA & ISHA SINHA 2021

Originally published in India

ISBN: 978-93-91041-58-8

Published by RIGI PUBLICATION

Printer: Manipal Printers

777, Street no.9, Krishna Nagar

Khanna-141401 (Punjab), India

Website: www.rigipublication.com

Email: info@rigipublication.com

Phone: +91-9357710014, +91-9465468291

ACKNOWLEDGEMENT

This novel is written by us but there are various hidden faces who contributed a lot in our journey.

First of all, we would like to thank my (Vaibhav's) Professor of Accounts: **Anurag Mishra**, who helped us in publishing and supported me throughout this journey.

Then we would like to thank various critics and proofreaders who helped us in identifying our plot or character shortcomings.

They are:
Ms M Sushma Shree (creative philosophical writer),

Shreya Choudhary, Devanshi Solanki, Rachit Shah, Varsha Chopra (school friends),

Somnath Nag (Professor of English),

Parshat Desai (innovations and business blogger),

Bhavya Logar (Dear sister), and Komal Agrawal.

We are grateful for the time and efforts you invested in our novel.

At last we want to thank our parents and siblings who supported us in our Journey.

This novel wouldn't have been possible without them.

INDEX

INTRODUCTION

*"This novel is dedicated to the unrecognised sacrifices of our mothers, especially you Mom (**Rekha Logar**). Whatever I'm today, it's because of you. Thank You Moms for making us what we are!"*

Everyone wants to imagine the future for their business ventures, job and career prospects, and family planning but no-one is able to envision the future properly. In this novel, I (Vaibhav Logar) have showcased my imagination of the future: The 24th Century. This book not only has a thrilling war plot and pure love story, but also Philosophies which if everyone of us may implement in our present life then we'll create an amazing future together. I hope you'll like my imagination, be fascinated towards the future innovations and implement the moral teachings in your life to be a happier version of yourself.

Story starts with Leo (a teenager in 2021) who accidently travels to the 24th century where he makes new friends and falls in love with a girl named Mary. Fascinated by learning innovative business ideas of the future, Leo gets emotionally connected with Mary as the time passes. Their relationship faces various hurdles and no-one can predict "Will the love souls unite or not". This Love story runs parallely with War plot to make you feel thrill and love at the same time.

You will not be able to stop crackling on Sahil's puns and Commander's strictness will keep on reminding you, your strict parent or professor. You will have butterflies in your stomach with further advancement of the War-plot and unanticipated twists and turns. You'll feel pity, excited, depressed, helpless, rejoiced, in love, and various other emotions as you progress with the story.

Finally, after completing this story, even at your work-place or at your home, you'll be lost in the 24th Century. You'll again recall this day when you're starting your journey in future and you'll feel grateful for it."
So, All The Best for your journey. For you, The Future awaits .

CHAPTER 1
THE TIME-TRAVEL

"We have to get through this small opening into the future to save the world, otherwise we will lose not only our earth, but the complete universe.... or even the multiverse" Somebody said.......

I am sweating, heavily breathing, not knowing whether I will make it or not, this is the question of all of humanity, my hands are shaking, blood is running from my knees, my heart is beating at a very fast pace, air is passing from my ears, I'm hearing the feeble voices of my loved ones who are saying that I can do this...... But suddenly I'm able to see a pigeon passing near my spaceship, who is saying wake-up bro...... wake-up broooooo.......

"Come on, you have slept 15 hours, and what's the matter with the spaceship... I think you saw the same dream again of saving humanity" my sister, Nitya, yelled.. and laughed

I woke up with heavy breathes, and as usual I freshened up. After doing my breakfast, I again got back in a resting position as I've no work to do.

"Life has grown boring," I thought aloud as I sat on the porch looking at the grey sky. "And somewhat meaningless."

It felt like I spent most of my time cooped up in my room with online classes, courtesy of Coronavirus. As I grew accustomed to this lazy lifestyle, the dream I had of becoming a world renowned scientist and a successful entrepreneur, a responsible citizen, and a national patriot seemed to be drifting further and further away.

I scooped up the snow that had piled up on the grass with my gloved hand and started shaping it into a ball.

My future seemed bleak. Would I just end up becoming an average income person, will I create no difference in society. These all questions made me heavy and worried.

No matter what I did, it was hard to take these online classes seriously. My grades were getting worse by the day. With so little contact I had grown apart from my friends and I feel like we barely even talk.

I remember when we used to roam around the city, playing pranks on strangers, playing sports, making fun of each other and teachers. Those were such good days, we went multiple times to watch movies and create wonderful memories. From watching the movie to the gossip and jokes in between a physical lecture, the relaxation in the travel to tourist destinations to dancing in various functions, I really miss all of that so badly, but what can we do there is no option.

I walked past the wooden fence that separated my house from the woods. With all the force I could muster, I threw the snowball at the trunk of a tree and chuckled as it exploded.

As I watched my breath solidify in the cold, I heard an annoying voice. "What's with the pensive mood?" My sister called. She was supposed to be three years older than me, but acted like she was three. Further proving my belief, she shoved my shoulder.

I shoved her as well. But with the force of a growing adolescent boy that I was, she fell to the ground. I chuckled at her and her face twisted with anger. I saw that a maroon scarf that my mother had knitted for my sixteenth birthday three months ago fell to the ground and got wet from the snow. "My butt's frozen because of you!" She yelled.

I stuck out my tongue at her and rushed towards the woods before she could retaliate. I could hear her footsteps chasing after me, but as I ran further and further, her footsteps seemed to be fading away.

I looked behind and saw no trace of her. "That's odd," I mumbled. Nitya would never leave a chance at revenge and fat as she was, she was surprisingly quick on her feet. She should have caught up to me by now.

I was about to go back home, but was stopped by a beeping sound behind me.

As soon as I tried to look deeper into the wood, I had to cover my eyes as a blinding flash of light shot at me. It started causing me a headache.

I stood there along with a stick but suddenly the flash of light receded, and then my headache faded away as well. Too scared to check out the source, I started walking back to my house.

My stride was slow paced as I tried to contemplate what had happened. I looked up at the sky, but it wasn't grey anymore, which was odd considering it was the middle of December and it was usually impossible to see a clear sky at this time of the year in Manali.

My feet and my heart both stopped as I looked down. "No..." I mumbled. "No. No. This can't be happening."

My feet moved on their own. Instead I would say they were flying towards a big spaceship in the sky. "Papa!" I yelled. "Didi! Mom!" My throat itches with how hard I screamed and tears kept streaming down my eyes as I kept calling out to my family.

My throat grew sore from crying and screaming, but I didn't... couldn't stop yelling for my family. I was just flying towards the spaceship and recalling the glimpses from sci-fi movies, I thought it was an alien spaceship.

The nausea took over me and I felt my hands trembling uncontrollably. With a sharp pain in my head, I got unconscious and the last thing I saw was getting into that spaceship and my last words were, "Don't worry, it is just a dream...", but I know somehow it's not only a dream…

CHAPTER 2
IN THE SPACESHIP

"Wake up! Wake up."

I blinked my eyes as I heard muffled voices. I looked around and grief overcame me all over again as I realized it was not a dream. I rubbed my eyes and looked around. I was in a small room with walls that looked like beds. Like the ones in mental wards for critical patients. I saw a robot in front of me. And not one of those made of nothing but metal, but one that looked like a human if you didn't look too closely. However, it was obvious to me as wires from the tablet it held were attached to it's inner arm. It wore nothing but black clothes.

It made some chattering noises and at my confused look it started speaking something that seemed like a legitimate language.
Robot said, "Jaglib 001091 jaligba"

"I still don't understand."

It's cold gaze looked at me with a knowing look and finally asked me in a language I understand.

"Are you hurt," it's voice was cold and mechanical. I shook my head.

"Who are you?" I asked with a sore voice.

"I am called AL79. I am an AI from the health unit."
The AI touched the tablet it held and asked, "What's your name?"

"My... name?" I thought for a moment. "What is my name?" I panicked. I sat up straight and clutched my head as a sharp pain went through it. "I can't remember."

It took out what looked like a pen from one of its pockets and raised it right in front of my nose. "Focus your eyes on it's tip," he said.

I did as I was told. "Slight trembling," It said, putting the pen away. "You have been diagnosed with 4D Amnesia."

"What?"

Before I could react, it pulled out a syringe from one of its pockets and injected me with a suspicious looking green liquid.

"What the hell did you just inject me with?"

"It would ease your headaches. Do you know what the fourth dimension is?" It asked putting a hand on my shoulder.

Baffled by the sudden question, I still answered. "Time?"

"You have just traveled through the fourth dimension. Could you tell
me what year are you from?" It asked before I could even let the world changing facts sink in.

"2021," I said.
"So... where am I now, are you all aliens?" I screamed

"You should probably ask when you are (It's 2340)."
"2340?", I yelled.

"Indeed.", the robot said.

"So... this is a time machine?"

"Yes."

"Poor guy. He was probably caught up in the extended radius of the time machine and came here."

I looked at the entrance and watched as two girls about my age entered. One had a long black braid. And the other had a blond Bob cut.

"A foreigner..." I mumbled.
"Foreigner? Where?" The black haired girl asked, looking around.
I pointed at the blonde. The girl squinted her eyes at me. She is obviously human, why would you call her a foreigner?"

The girl seemed to be timid and hid behind the black haired girl. "So let me introduce myself", said the black haired girl, "I'm Jessie, from the 24th century, I'm twenty two, Commander of URJA. This," she said pointing at the blond girl, "is Mariana, she is sixteen, our group's most reliable weapons specialist and Artificial intelligence master. She is a little shy but once you get to know her, she will prove to be the most loving and adorable creature you can ever meet in your life. We are from the 24th century and when we were in your timeline for some work, we accidentally dragged you along." I looked at the two. Confusion and disbelief, clear as day, were on my face.

"Anyway, what's your name, kid?" Jessie asked.

I looked down in embarrassment, "I'm…… umm sorry I don't remember my name, I can't remember anything."

The robot said, "Because of unprotected time travel, this human
the child has forgotten everything. Mere glimpses of his past might
be safe in his mind right now, however we predict his age to be
somewhere between 16 to 18."

Mariana said in an empathetic tone, "Don't worry, we will find a
cure for it and will safely escort you back in your time."

I glanced at the Mariana and was unable to take my eyes off of her.
Her elegant demeanor and soft voice made it easy for anyone to get
attracted to her. Her hair was bright like gold and as her straight
strands fell on her face, it gave her an enchanting look. Her skin
seemed as smooth as silk, like she was a porcelain doll, her cheeks
a rosy pink. Her smile could make even the most aloof of men smile
back

She was really like an angel that had descended from heaven. I felt
like I had already fallen hard for her.

She was staring right back at me. Even though she was almost a
meter apart from me, I could feel that we were slowly drawing
closer. As if relishing that she had been staring at me, she tried to
hide her blushing cheeks behind her hands. I tried to hide my own
blush for it was the cutest thing I have ever seen.

Despite my anxiousness and nervousness I wanted to tell her that
she is beautiful but before I could get a word in, Jessie interrupted,
"It would be better if you know more about this timeline now itself,
as you could be staying here for a while after all. Right now, we are
in the midst of an intergalactic war." That statement brought me
back to reality.
"A war?" I choked.

"Indeed. The group we are in is called URJA."

"A war….. ohh God, I remember reading about two world wars in my history books. Our professors said that if a third World War were to take place, it would be the end of humanity. We are in grave danger, aren't we?"

Jessie in a calm voice said, "I understand your curiosity and your concern for the present, but the present is far beyond your imagination. Don't worry, Mary can you show this kid around," Mariana gave a nod.

Jessie looked back at me. "She will brief you about what happened after twenty twenty-one, isn't it?" I gave her a nod. "Take him to your lab after you are finished with the tour. We can't have him dragging us down in an invasion."

Jessie looked at me and said in a serious tone, "Sorry kid, we can't take you back to your time for we are a little tight on time, right now. I have to leave to manage my squad and be prepared to set out back to the future earth of the 24th century."

Mariana said, "it seems I shall be your mentor , for now..." and she smiles.

Oh, her smile. It made me crazy. I got the feeling like I was watching the most beautiful waterfall from the top or watching the entire world from the mountain top. It was a moment to treasure in my heart. I said, "Yeah, I am looking forward to it....." I smiled.

We had toured through a majority of the time-machine before we reached her lab. It was really amazing. The clothes they wore, the interior architecture, the A.I. Robots going here and there, everything was driving me crazy and every passing second a new questions rose in my mind.

Finally we reached her lab, apart from the actual tech, everything in the room was white. The lab was filled with too much tech and amazing weapons, weapons I had never seen in my timeline from what little I remembered of it. I get glimpses of my timeline weapons which were guns, bombs, etc. but these are very different.
Mariana said, "So, did you like the time machine?"

I said, "Absolutely, it's fantastic." Now that I had spent some time with Mariana, I could feel the burst of hormones from earlier slowly receding. I could finally have a normal conversation with her , without my heart about to burst out. It is just like being somewhat familiar with your crush and now talking to her just as you talk to a friend.

I asked, "can I also call you marry, ohh sorry I mean Mary?."
She firstly laughed and then gave a nod. We finally reached her lab where I asked, "Can you tell me more about the future, what happened from my century to yours?"

She after thinking for some time said, "Alright, so it's really difficult from where to start, but let me start from explaining about the internet of the 1990s. After the industrial revolution of the 1850s, another breakthrough innovation which changed the entire world was the internet. It gave humanity access to many things, which seemed impossible before, the internet connected the world and made it a global village."
What she said made sense, after all, only my memories had been tampered with, not my knowledge, if that were the case, I would

even remember to speak. But I didn't interrupt her since I loved listening to her voice."Yeah, but can you explain further about the internet as I can't remember much."

Mary started again in a very sweet voice, "The Internet gave birth to new innovative companies like Facebook and WhatsApp of our time, which have connected billions of people from various corners of the world. Google was also a very popular name, which gave a new shape to reading news, watching our favourite videos through YouTube owned by Google, Google maps which helped to get to our desired location anytime without any problem. Then between 2010 to 2020, various startups used internet and business innovative ideas to solve various problems of society, some include OLA and UBER which brought convenience in booking a taxi ride, then Amazon which started the e-commerce journey and connected various businesses with consumers, then come the online food ordering apps (Zomato, Doordash, Grubhub, etc.), then the edtech apps (Byju's, Coursera, Khan Academy). This way the Internet will change the lives of many people till 2020."

I remembered all these familiar names and said, "Yeah, I have heard the names of these companies." although I'm no longer crazy for her, but her voice is really making me even more attracted towards her.

Mary continues, "Then when covid came in 2019, it boosted the digitalisation in the world even further. It was a really bad time because of it as far as I have heard about lockdowns and death but by 2025, the covid became a normal flu, as almost everyone was vaccinated so the strength of the virus was no longer affecting the human immune system. Then after the covid got over, there started the best time of humanity."
I was overwhelmed with curiosity and asked, "How??"

"Come on, sweetie, have some patience," Mary teased. This sentence gave me goosebumps. I objected to Jessie's statement where she said that Mary was shy as she is getting open with me, I liked this and smiled.

Mary continued, "covid led to amazing growth of the digital world, many new startups and innovative ideas come around the internet. Even between 2020 to 2050, the world saw a very big rise in new innovative technologies, some of which are blockchain, A.I, Green energies, quantum technology, Electric Vehicles, Space exploration techniques, etc,...." Mary suddenly stopped.

"What is it?"

"I would like to explain more but I am unsure of how much I should reveal to a person from the past. There are some restrictions regarding the things we humans can share with the previous generations. But let me check the restrictions once, I will be right back." With that she left the room.

In the room, there was a photo of her along with another person, I moved forward to see it closely but as I was walking towards it, I got I had to jerk back for alarms in the time machine had started buzzing, and loud noises from outside the room started coming. Some people said aloud, "There is an attack on us, run, run, and go outside the room."
I became frightened and ran outside the room into the lobby of time machine.

CHAPTER 3
THE FUTURE INNOVATIONS

When I reached the main lobby of the time machine the havoc had spread all over. Everyone was panic stricken as chaos took over the ship. When Jessie finally appeared she yelled in a stern voice, "there's no need to piss your pants just yet, the time machine is just stuck in sometime. There is no attack."

After Jessie's hearing Jessie's words everyone relaxed, relief evident on their faces and started going back to their rooms, cabins, labs or wherever they needed to be, but I was still confused and just stood there in a daze until Mary came to me.

Mary tapped my shoulder, "why are you here, I told you to wait in my lab."

Looking at my expression, she sighed and grabbed my wrist, "You don't have to worry. Like Jessie said, it wasn't some attack, there was just some technical issue with the time machine. It will be repaired soon and then we can go back to our time. I have to ask Jessie when are we going to leave you in your time...."

Jessie suddenly appeared in front of us and beckoned Mary to follow her. "Excuse me for a moment," she mumbled and left with her superior. I stood there like an obedient child, unable to hear their discussion.

"I talked with the Commander about the boy and he said that we can't drop him back in his time now as he has lost his memory and we don't know if just dropping him back will bring his memory back. The commander has pledged to take responsibility, as it was our mistake to get him in our time machine; it is our duty to bring his memory back." Said Jessie to Mary and I'm not able to hear it.

Mary looked back at the boy and mumbled, "I completely agree with him and I will try my best to bring his memory back by talking with him about the 21st century. I hope this method works, as psychology is one of my 5 areas of specialization."

"I believe in you Mary, I will order someone else to help you out." said Jessie as she crossed her arms. "But take care so that he never feels disheartened, make him comfortable and treat him like a part of our family."

I wonder what they are talking about? War strategy, their studies, the food...... ugh, I wish I knew how to read lips. It's really hard to guess just by standing here and watching their mouths move.

I kicked the air and fiddled with my fingers as I waited for Mary to come back.

"Come on, let's go back to my lab where I will tell you further about what happened in the complete 21st and 22nd century." Said Mary.

Mary suddenly started speaking "ummm.... is it really that important?... I'm with a boy from the 21st century right now, so can we talk later...."

I blinked at Mary's sudden out of context words as she started talking to thin air. She wasn't talking to me as she was looking here and there but there was no-one around which made me frightened.

I thought in my head, "Could it be that she was mentally challenged, she may be a psycho who hallucinated, and I was attracted to a psycho……,or is it really my dream, a ghostly dream."
I took a couple of steps away from her. When she looked at me with a confused expression, I said, "Hey, are u ok. Do you need me to bring you your meds? Should... should I call a doctor?"

I looked at her face twisting with an array of emotions. I took another step away from her.

"I will talk to you later. I have something to deal with right now," she mumbled and took a step toward me. I too stepped backwards and felt myself backed up against a wall.

"Why are you asking so teenager, What happened," Mary said as she pressed a hand against my chest and drew closer.

"S- stay away from me, You suddenly started speaking to someone who wasn't visible….. a characteristic of mentally ill patient…." I cried.

Mary looked at me with a raised brow for a long second and then started laughing like she had heard something crazy. I got even more frightened, wondering if her circuit had completely crashed. I started calling others for help, "Please help me and Mary……. is this machine cursed by ghosts.... ohh man, please help..." I cried.

Mary laughed harder at my jumbled words and while still in a fit of laughter, said, "Hey, don't worry, I am fine, I'm not a psycho.... I'm a normal human with a sound mind. What you saw was a nano-tech device which people from your time called cell phone," she chuckled.

But wasn't a cell phone supposed to be a big device, through which we could call people, but still confused I wondered aloud, "where is the phone?"

Mary explained in a very simple manner with her beautiful accent and cute hand actions (Just moments earlier I thought she was a psycho, but now again her voice, personality and cute smile made me believe that I was the psycho to ever think of her as a psycho),

"This phone was invented in the 22nd century. In this a small nano-tech device is fitted near your eardrum and is connected with your brain, using special connection Arizona (similar to wifi), if I want to call someone, I have to just think of their name and the call is automatically placed and I'm able to hear it directly without any outside device being required. This device is fitted near the eardrum just after the birth of a child. There are many technologies which will blow your mind, but first let's go to my lab."

On the way back, I just kept thinking about this **nano-phone**, "does it make your ear itch?" I asked, wondering if it ever felt uncomfortable.

Mary chuckled, "What a cute question." I blushed, embarrassed by her reaction. "No, it doesn't itch. And besides, even though this is something we have had our whole lives, it's something we are used to." She said as if she had read my mind.

"But is it even safe to keep such technology so close to your brain. What if it glitched or something?"

"Well... if that were the case, the person wearing it would die." I gulped at the statement. "But then again, it never happened since it was made public after a lot of experimentation, and even monthly, we have to visit ear doctors to clean and examine this device."

I thought for a moment, "Nice," I mumbled.

Then we reached Mary's lab, she leaned against a wall and looked at me with a sad expression, "so, uhh, now listen carefully. As you are from the 21st century and lost your memories, we can only send you back when you retrieve them." I looked at her for a moment then lowered my head after I felt a sting in my eyes.

"I see.", I got somewhat sad to hear that I have lost my memories.

"Don't worry!" Mary said as she rubbed my arm. "We will make your memories come back. I promise." I gave her a nod and as if giving me some time to collect myself..

"Anyway," she started after a while. "I will share some innovations which had already started or had been thought of by someone in your time, if I tell you about the ones which are of a later time like the 22nd century, and you discuss those with your family and friends and those ideas are completed before their time, then it might change the present. And you know the laws of time travel. You do not mess with the past, you do not affect the present."

I looked at her with a serious expression.

Mary said, "You can think of it as some ideas of your future, I can share some of them with you and some I can't, in such a way that the future is not changed."
I nodded, "Ok, then let's begin."

Mary gave me a smile, punched in some numbers and letters on her computer and I watched as a hologram appeared over it. Mary smirked as I gawked at it in awe.

She looked at me and started, "From 2010, the global era of startups began. Many new business ideas came, which solved many problems of people and society. From 2020 to 2050, startups even increased and they were made to solve various problems of our daily life, or they introduced some new technology in the market. So mostly the economy from 2020 to 2090 is called in today's world **The startups era**. Now let me explain, what kind of startups have been made in this time-period and other innovations in various industries."

Mary said a voice command and a 3-d hologram type ppt popped out.

Mary started, "The most revolutionary technologies which shaped the 21st and 22nd century were the Internet and Blockchain. The Internet connected everyone and Blockchain secured that connection. As I have already explained to you various startups of the internet era, let me start by explaining some mind-blowing innovations with Blockchain. First of all, Blockchain revolutionized the Financial industry as banking transactions happened with Blockchain tech, making them secured, easy, transparent, and quick. After 2030, most banks, NBFCs started changing their payment, deposit and lending systems with Blockchain tech."

Mary continued, "Then Blockchain tech transformed the Power sector, as everyone started adopting Green Energy from 2015, and from 2040 Green Energy was harnessed in every home with the help of nano-tech solar panels. Here Blockchain helped in distribution in the following way; The amount of Green energy produced by every household got stored in a database with the help of Blockchain and then the usage of power was calculated in the same way. This helped the Government to determine which area/City/State contributed more Green energy and similarly made plans to harness more energy from there. Blockchain helped to use data in a more effective and secure way."

"Similarly Blockchain was used to protect important documents, Nuclear codes, etc. This way Blockchain was used in various industries, the rest of which I can't tell to prevent the future from changing."

I got fascinated by listening about Blockchain and started recalling a familiar term…. I said to her, "Bitcoin, have you heard this term anywhere."

She said with a smile depicting genuine happiness, "Yes. Bitcoin was the first currency which used Blockchain tech. I think our discussion is helping to bring your memories back."

I was really grateful to her, making such an effort for an unknown person and said, "Thank You very much for your help."

Mary smiled and continued, "so… now let's continue to the agriculture sector." She showed me vast lands of crops growing in the hologram.

"Till 2025, the agro-sector was very unorganized and unprofitable. Farmers were mostly poor because of it, corruption had completely taken over their lives, leading to poor situations for farmers."

I could see tiny little men reaping crops with nothing but knives.

"But from 2025, situations will start to change, and the agro-sector went through digitalisation."

Mary swiped the hologram and everything in it changed. It showed farmers using cell phones and complex machines were tilling the crops.

"In 2025, startups came which created an online platform (**Agro-India platform**) for farmers with which farmers can sell their fresh-farm produce directly to consumers and households who want direct fresh veggies from farms. This platform became so popular that most of the country's farmers sell their produce through it and get very good returns as this platform cuts the commission of middlemen, agents and other parties."

She swiped it upward and a screen popped out like a window in a computer and it looked like some website. She swiftly swiped up. If the screen had been smaller, it would have looked like she had been scrolling down in an app on her cell phone. It can be imagined as a ppt in 3D like it:-

"In the 2030s, **blockchain technology was applied in agriculture*** which further improved the conditions of the agro-sector and solved various problems of manipulating transactions, charging higher prices, and helped in digitalising the Agro-sector.

Mary seemed to have caught my dazed look and asked, "Hey are you listening, boy??"

I uttered, "Can I have a name, as being called but a pronoun doesn't always sound good."

She continued with a smile, " I have thought about your name problem, we can assign a nicl-name to you, until your real name flashes in your memory…… so as you are sweet, kind-hearted and appear in our time-machine just as a ray of light or a star, so I'm thinking of naming you LEO….. How's it??"

I smiled as Mary understood me and thought of me as a kind and sweet person…. saying, "Yeah, I liked this one..".

"Mary was good-looking and beautiful as I firstly saw her because of which I got butterflies in my stomach but now as I'm developing a bond with her, I'm not attracted to her outer body but to her beautiful heart, who cares about a person from past without even knowing whereabouts of his, who understands people, their pain, their happiness, etc.. This is really a very rare quality." I thought while speaking.

I was really astonished at what I had heard and seen today. I said, "Mary, it's really mind- blowing, did the work on this idea start in 2021?"

Mary said, "No, it is still not thought of by anyone. It will become a business opportunity after 2 to 3 years when new entrepreneurs will think of it."

After thinking this I humorously said, "What if I take this idea and start my own startup, it will change the future, right...." I laughed.

Mary got serious instead of laughing and said, "A startup is not easy to establish, it doesn't only need a business idea but it requires patience, courage, optimism, vision, hope and the most important sacrifices. The ones I am sharing with you are only those ideas which are either very difficult to start in 2021 therefore, if someone started any similar startup, it may not succeed."

"But then too, you are welcome to try when you go back....." She smiled and continued,

With another swipe at the hologram everything changed completely. There were crops in broad daylight, now the consumables were planted in what looked like caves, plagued with darkness. The only source of light were the ones that looked like light used in a concert, incredibly bright (red and blue, instead of white) and directed right at the... black leaves.

Mary continued, "Then in the 2050s, another breakthrough innovation came in the agro Sector, where many countries started **Underground Farming** in which under the ground, the plants and crops are grown with the help of artificial sunlight, and proper irrigation systems."

I asked, "Is it really possible, to grow plants underground, I never thought of it... but why are the leaves black?"

"Oh that.... well. Plants don't need green light, that's why they appear green, because they reflect it back. Therefore in the underground agriculture, farmers, who were also scientists and businessmen, only used red and blue light, there was no green light to reflect back, so plants looked black." Mary smiled, "and everything is possible, if you imagine it, believe it and then achieve it." The next hologram was however much more unprecedented than the earlier ones. Because below the diagram... it was labeled **'MARS SETTLEMENT'**

"M... Mars?" I mumbled, completely amazed.

Mary chuckled at my outburst and said, "at the end of 21st century, many planets of our solar system were made suitable to our lifeform, agriculture was done in various areas of those planets and it even became completely automated by that time, robots and artificial intelligence does most of the part and there was no physical labours required."

She swiped through some holograms of settlements from different planets... and soon the manual labourers were completely replaced by robots. Shooting beams of light from their hands, sprinkling water from their... unmentionables. I looked at Mary, she seemed to be holding in her laughter.

"Yeah... that happened." She chuckled.

I looked away, trying to suppress my own outburst. "The one who invented that must have some sick sense of humor." Mary snorted and changed the slide. She said," There were further innovations to calculate the rainfall, humidity, sunlight, moisture etc. in the agriculture sector as we can see in the slide":-

I said, "It's really amazing to see so many innovations, business ideas in the agri-sector... which is often considered by many individuals a sector which can't grow and change with time.. But the future proved that these assumptions are wrong. There can be development anywhere at any time."

Mary smiled and said, "Very true Leo..."

I smiled and asked, "Thanks and Anything else on agro....?"
Mary said, "No, for the time being that's it for the agro-sector, now I hope you liked my IOT clothes..." She said as she kept a hand on her waist, striking a pose as if she were pretending to be a model. That said, she was pretty enough to be one.

But... I looked at her with a confused look and thought yeah clothes are good and she looks beautiful in them but what was Iot??

Finally, after racking my brains for a minute, I asked, "what's IOT?"

Mary smiled, typed something on her computer, then said, "Then let me start by explaining the Textile sector. After 2025, many innovations started coming in textiles. The most important was **Textile Recycling Concept***."

The hologram showed a pair of old jeans being dumped into a machine and I saw it tearing it into threads and remodeling it into another, though a bit shorter pair of jeans.

"In this concept, old textiles were recycled and got converted to completely new textile clothes, with no change in quality. For eg: From your old jeans, you can make new jeans of same quality, same colour but its price will get halved as there was no use of new raw materials. This made good quality textile clothes very cheap such that even poors can afford them and reduced wastage which was a very environmentally friendly move. It changed the textile industry."

Mary sat down on a chair nearby, resting her elbow on her desk and her head on the back of her hand. I watched as her short blond hair fell on her face and she quickly tucked it behind her ear.

I gave her a glass of water and she started again. Though I persuaded her to wait and relax, she insisted that she was not tired. I further got impressed by her dedication.

"Then the most mind-blowing innovation of the textile industry was **IOT Clothes(Internet Of Things)** which came in the 2060s, where your clothes got connected to the internet, they were made from electronic fibres but felt the same as cotton or silk. In it, your T-shirt can measure the rate of you heartbeat, your oxygen level, even by tapping on your chest, a hologram will emerge out which will look exactly like a laptop's screen and you can text, call anyone, search anything on Google, it has other features too, but I can't tell you of IOT clothes because of the restrictions as I told you before, to prevent future from changing."

The photo from the slide looked like this :-

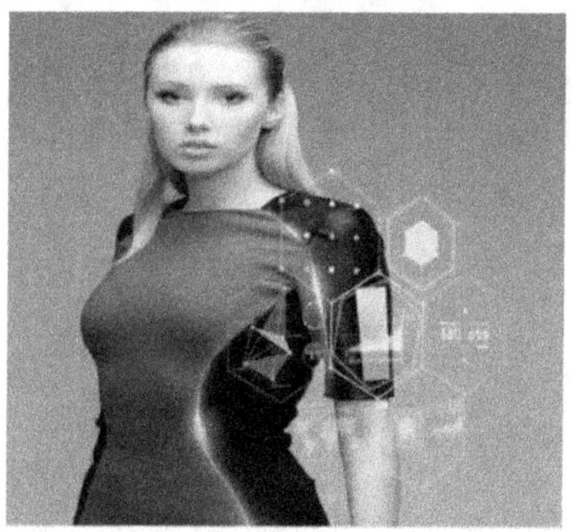

Mary continued, "Apart from clothes, IOT was applied in a number of industries. Everyone's home, furniture and all appliances were connected to the Internet by 2050 and became Smart Homes. In Smart homes, your lights, T.V., A.C., Microwave, Sofa, and other appliances were accessible through your phone, you can turn them on/off just by a click in your phone. Even in hospitals, beds, medical equipment were connected with each other by IOT. Similarly, streets, gardens, footpaths, police stations, etc. all became a part of the IOT infrastructure of the city. This way cities gradually changed to smart cities because of the Internet Of Things:-

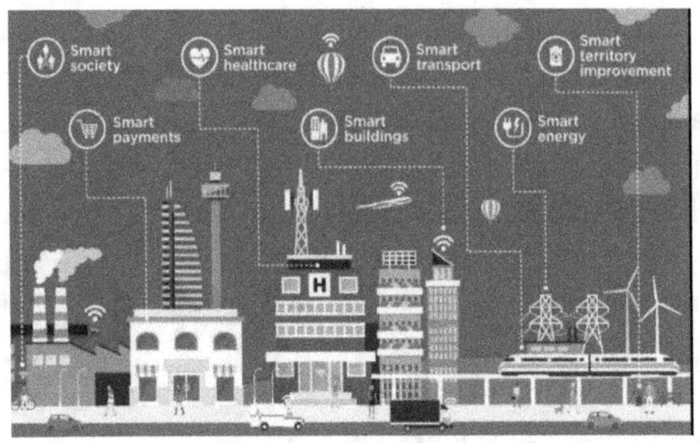

"Everything about the future is really mind blowing" I got ecstatic after listening to this. I never thought future tech could be so beautiful, it really made me overwhelmed with joy to see such an incredible future.

"Hey Mary! It's been a while," I turned to see a black haired boy in a black IOT jacket walk toward us.

"Sahil! What are you doing here? I thought you had your training class right-" Mary was cut short when Sahil drew her into a hug. Mary chuckled, "what's up with you?"

"Nothing, just routine work and development activities….. and now just chill chit-chat with you" he whined.

"Ohhh? Just for that you came here.." Mary asked with a raised brow.

"Yeah! And guess what? I heard rumors that Jessie put you in charge of him!! Mary, tell me that is not true... please.

Mary chuckled and pushed him away from her, playfully punched his arm and said, "I could say that, but then I would be lying. Check him out."

Sahil fixed his eyes on me as if he were scanning me. "Shit, you are good looking. Can things get any worse."

Mary flicked Sahil's forehead, "ow!"

How playful Mary was with him, and with the smile spread across her face, I couldn't help but wonder if they were dating. Don't tell me this would be the end of our.... my one sided crush.

"I guess introductions are in order," Mary said and pointed at Sahil as if he were some product on display that she was promoting. "This is Sahil, one of our elite combatants. He is also responsible for teaching the kids to fend for themselves in times of a cease-fire like now. Apart from that, he is the most compassionate and humorous person of our team."

Now I was the product on display, "This is the boy who accidentally traveled through time with us. His name.... we don't know that yet. But I call him LEO"

"Ooh friend LEO, don't feel awkward here…. We are all just friends with an age gap of 200 to 300 years."

Everyone laughed including me.

 Sahil continued, "But age is just a number. We all have the same hearts. That is a kind one…. Though some day, some of us will be

your great-grandchildren, but no issue at present we are just friends."
Again everyone laughed.

As Sahil talked so much about being friends, I asked, " So are you both also friends or bf-gf??"

Sahil said, " Ohh Mary, now I think we have to inform him…. Truly saying to you Leo, I'm Mary's bf.."

My heart stopped for a moment… But Sahil continued and said, "I'm her bf with an additional "f" in it…. So, I'm her bff (Best Friend Forever) and she is the same to me..."

Mary and Sahil laughed and I firstly restarted my heart and joined them in laughter...

An awkward silence settled between us then.

Mary, intent on clearing the air of the tension, looked me over and asked, "Are you hungry, let's order some food. I think you will like burgers as in your time, it was a very popular dish."
I said "Yeah sure. A veg burger should be fine. So, can you even tell me about the innovations of the food industry by the time food comes?" I asked.

The food, however, popped out on the table within 2 seconds....

"What the-?" I jumped away from my seat when I saw a perfectly grilled burger appear out of thin air, "Are you kidding me."

Mary and Sahil laughed first. Then Mary said, "I will explain as we eat...."

I yelled, "Yeah please..... I'm already dumbstruck with what just happened..."

Mary laughed and continued, "Now talking about the food industry, after the food delivery apps innovations, in the 2030s, a very new concept got extremely popular. The concept of **Cloud kitchens** changed the business environment of small restaurants and fast food."

Sahil swiped the hologram to show a kitchen with an assortment of dishes being cooked in it.

"In it, as most people got very familiar with ordering food online and eating at home, the restaurants no longer required seats, staff, etc. They just needed a kitchen and this way they could save a lot of money. So many small restaurant owners thought that if we jointly own a big kitchen in which we can divide its space among us, and each of us could make our food and give it to the delivery personnel then it would further reduce the cost (as rents will be shared collectively by all restaurant owners), will improve efficiency (as various chefs of different restaurants will work together and make dishes), and even we could maintain good hygiene conditions."

"So, even the most famous Indian dish panipuris, which all Indians love, but was prepared in unhygienic conditions got the most benefit from it. As various pani puri-walas and other chat (fast-food sellers) come together and rent a big kitchen, in which they divide the kitchen space among themselves and make their dishes with proper hygiene and then deliver it to their customers."

"This event led to entrepreneurial innovations in this stall food business, as they improved packaging in such a way that in case of pani-puri, the customers can enjoy the same taste as they would if they come out on stall, even pani-puris became healthy as organic materials were used in proper hygiene space to make it," Sahil explained before he dug his teeth into a piece of pastry.
"This way, what no-one could have ever thought in 2021, **a pani-puri making and selling company made by various pani-puri walas, got listed in India's stock exchange in 2032.** The innovations they brought in the food space was really mind-blowing, and it again taught the world a very important entrepreneurial lesson (Innovations can be done in any sector, any business, by anyone)," Mary said.

I don't know why, but I felt a little proud that she could make an example of an Indian dish, despite the fact that she was a foreigner.

"OMG, Now really, I just wish that when I get back in 2021, this future may come very soon, I can see it and be amazed by this whole innovation." I said after completing my burger and cleaning the cheese which dripped down from my lips as I listened to all this and forgot to close my mouth.

Mary laughed, "Yeah, you will surely see this. Then when teleporters were invented in the beginning of the 22nd century, again the transportation system got disrupted, and your burger was also teleported from the time-machine kitchen."

"It's like... wow" I said as I didn't have any further words to describe such innovations. "Can humans also be teleported by this?" I asked out of curiosity.

"Of course" I heard, but it wasn't Mary's voice.

"Who said that?" I asked Mary.

Suddenly, someone appeared in front of us in the attire of a samurai and said, "Your days are over, destiny may have brought you here. But now, you must die for you have seen my face," saying that, he took out his sword and put it right at my neck."

"I gulped. Why me? I wondered as I squeezed my eyes shut with fear. His look alarmed us.

CHAPTER 4

IMPACT OF ARTIFICIAL INTELLIGENCE

Never before have I been as horrified I was as at that moment. I yelled, "What have I done? Who are you...?" I mumbled as I tried to look for a place to hide myself from the impending danger. "Mary, Sahil please help!"

Mary was still as a statue, but Sahil finally gathered up enough courage to speak and said, "what do you want?" His tone reminded me of James Bond movies and I recalled that I used to watch those in my time.

The samurai swung his sword and spoke in his deep voice, "Your flesh, your blood, your heart.... I want them all. We are in a state of war. You can neither win nor can you run away. You all have to die."

The samurai rushed towards me with his long, shining and sharp blade. His sword was just near my neck and I thought that my life was about to end.

But suddenly Sahil asserted, "Let them go, and fight me instead. Don't you dare hurt my friends!"

I was very impressed by Sahil who was willing to sacrifice himself for me and Mary, despite the fact we had barely been acquainted. But the Samurai wasn't in the mood to listen to any nuisance, he was just about to strike his sharp sword's blade on my neck but Sahil rushed in front of me to save me.

Sahil said, "Please stop!... I know you don't want to hurt anyone. Stop."

The atmosphere in the lab was suffocating and terrifying. I could barely hold in the terror that was overtaking my whole body and my limbs were trembling with fear.

The samurai suddenly lowered his sword, Sahil slowly walked toward him to calm him down but he swiftly swung his sword, a whopping strike and just in a flick of seconds, I exclaimed, "What the fudge..."
I watched Sahil's body standing in front of the Samurai but his head flew near my legs, his eyes were open and blood was oozing out of his severed head... I screamed as hard as I could, tears started streaming down my cheeks.

Sahil.... he sacrificed his very life for me.... but... but there is nothing to stop the Samurai from killing Mary or me.

It was really the most terrifying moment of my life. I was completely helpless as I watched the death of a person who had barely become my friend.

I turned around to see Mary laughing. I wondered if Mary had lost her sanity. Why else would she be laughing at such a horrifying scene? I walked with small steps, small enough that the samurai, who was wiping Sahil's blood on the hem of his top, wouldn't notice and moved toward Mary. I grabbed her arm and said, "Mary control yourself, you can't go mad, you have to retain your sanity even at a time like this, we will find a way to solve this problem."

But Mary's laugh just got harder and harder. After a few minutes even the Samurai started laughing, not a villainous laugh but a mischievous normal one.

Now again, I was in a dilemma and I wasn't sure of what to say or think. How could a murderer laugh with such innocence, it really puzzled me. I mumbled under my breath, "Oh... God, what the heck is going on here."

"Woah! I never thought that a complete stranger would be so co concerned over my fall..." I turned around to the familiar voice....

"Sahil??"

Sahil chuckled, "Yup, it's me..." He chuckled again at my horrified expression.

"Look carefully that thing over there is my clone." Sahil said.

"A... clone?"

"It's just a clone, my friend, we played out a little dramatic- emphasis on the dramatic- scene just to give you some exciting and hilarious memories with your friends of the future..." he laughs.

Taking a moment to absorb the crazy antics of the Duo, I laughed with them after understanding how they tricked me. I said, "I really freaked out, don't ever do that again. But... nice work guys." I turned to Sahil's clone, "Is this really a clone, a biological individual organism that was grown from a single body cell of Sahil and is therefore genetically identical to Sahil?"

Sahil mused at my knowledge, "Yes, check it out yourself."

I looked closely at Sahil"s clone who was dead, it looked exactly like Sahil and when I was closely examining it, it suddenly disappeared. I said, "What happened, how did it disappear?"

Mary explained, "As in this complete drama, I was just standing aside doing absolutely nothing, allow me to explain what happened. Here in the 24th century, we make clones of us for various purposes and when such a wide use of clones started, we programmed each clone in such a way that it will disappear or will get decomposed to various micro particles invisible to human eye, after 20 to 30 minutes, so as to make sure that clones never become more powerful than humans. Therefore, Sahil played this trick along with Akito to have some fun. You can see that even Sahil's clone is decomposed now. Now Samurai, I think you must unmask yourself from this Samurai mask."

I looked at Sahil's clone and yes it got converted to dust.

Akito pulled down the piece of cloth covering his mask, "it was getting suffocating anyway." My eyes couldn't help but widen when he revealed his true face. The baggy clothes of a samurai shrunk to normal black IOT clothes.

He was the most handsome man I had ever seen. Even as a guy, I couldn't help but awe at the masterpiece he was.

Ohhh man! How can a person be so handsome with such an amazing physique. His eyes were blue with streaks of green making them more beautiful than Mary's or any other woman. His straight, thin nose and thin, beautiful lips may make me attracted to him. His strong chest, developed muscles, and a very strong core makes his physique one of the best in man's world. Though he was wearing clothes, I was sure he had 6 to 8 packs. If I were A girl, I wouldn't spare a second's hesitation to fall in love with him.

And now that the threat to my life was gone, I noticed how mesmerizing his deep voice was. If I didn't have any pride as a guy, I would have asked him to tell me a bedtime story with that voice of his.

Realizing that I had been staring at him for too long I turned away.

This was so weird, being a boy, I was fantasising about one. But really in terms of physique, he was second to none.

Mary started again, "So Leo met Akito. We usually call him AK, but this name is way too short to justify his personality. He is one of the smartest and most intelligent people in our group. He works directly under the commander and leads our group in his absence. His physique as you can see is also very good and at last he is compassionate and a little funny. But yeah I can say he is not as compassionate and funny as Sahil."

Sahil raised his chin as if proud of the compliment but modestly said, "Ohh... No no she is just flattering me."
He laughs and others too.

I laughed and at the same time thought, Mary described his qualities so passionately. I was sure that in my time, he could easily be the star of a movie, with all the girls fawning over his looks. Could Mary also be attracted or in love with him after having such qualities? Though as I heard them talking, it didn't look like they were in a relationship but maybe deep in their hearts love for eachother could be building.

Akito looked at me with a confused expression, "Hey... what are you thinking. Do you not like me?" He asked watching me.

I shook my head, "No... no. I was just so enchanted by your personality that I got lost."

Akito, "Ohh.. but I never like appraisal of my physique or intelligence. I think a person can be smart, and fit but to attain mental peace and happiness, he should be compassionate and understand others' pain and sufferings. He should love all the big and small creatures in his life and therefore even my aim in life is the same."
I was impressed by him, "It's an amazing ideal, I wonder what yhe world would be like if everyone was as caring as you."

Akito looked at Mary and asked, "Did you finish the work on the weapon which Commander assigned you to?"

Mary said, "Yes... It's outside, I will give it to you."

They both went out.

Left alone, my thought couldn't help but wander off to Mary's Relationship with Akito. I resolved myself not to be jealous of AK. He has a dashing personality. I like Mary and want her to be happy in her life but maybe she will not be as happy with me as with AK. She is perfect and she deserves someone perfect. Akito is better than me in all aspects, and I can never in my life overcome this cliff between us. He was too high up for me to even dream of reaching him. Maybe, I should just forget her. I could just be a good friend to her and will always be there when she needed my help.

In the middle of my self-depreciation, Sahil suddenly came right beside my ear and whispered, "You like Mary, Huh?" he laughed as jumped away from him. I completely forgot that he was in the room.

I said, "No.. of course not, why would you think that?"

Sahil smiles, "It is clear as day on your face. Your care for Mary and when Akito showed up, your jealousy when Mary was talking to AK, only an idiot wouldn't be able to see it. And since I am not an idiot for me, it was really easy to guess that this is nothing but love." I responded, "Well yes. You hit the bird's eye. Nice as Mary said, you are really empathetic, you can easily understand anyone's feelings. I wanted to be with her, I wanted to love her purely but she has a better companion and I don't think my happiness is of any worth as compared to her's."

Sahil explained, "My friend, feelings are not as simple as you think. Though, we are separated by centuries, but still even now, we are unable to make technology to determine feelings. You should not give up on your love, and for the first time ever, I have seen someone more empathetic and compassionate than me, as you are ready to sacrifice your happiness for your love bird's happiness. Its amazing. I can just hope that the upcoming circumstances come in favour of yours."

I said, "Thanks.. as Mary is not there now, so can you elucidate on what happened from my timeline to yours?"

Sahil started, "Yes sure. Many developments Mary has already explained to you. So now let me take innovations home. As you already know, we have inhabited other planets of the solar system apart from earth. We started settlements there in the 22nd century. Then to protect households from natural calamities, we made floating houses without water... in the air, it has gravity removing tech, and therefore when earth starts shaking because of an earthquake, the house rises in air. Like this...." He said, opening the holographic presentation.

"We used this tech even for settlements on other planets. Then in the 22nd and 23rd century, we mainly built IOT (Internet Of Things), as these homes are connected to the internet, listen to our voice commands, also there are sensors which automatically predict movements (like steps) and take necessary actions accordingly. Even in the 23rd Century, AI homes started building which can do all the necessary household work by itself. Then **VR (Virtual Reality)** also got added to homes, which made homes further interesting. See here:-

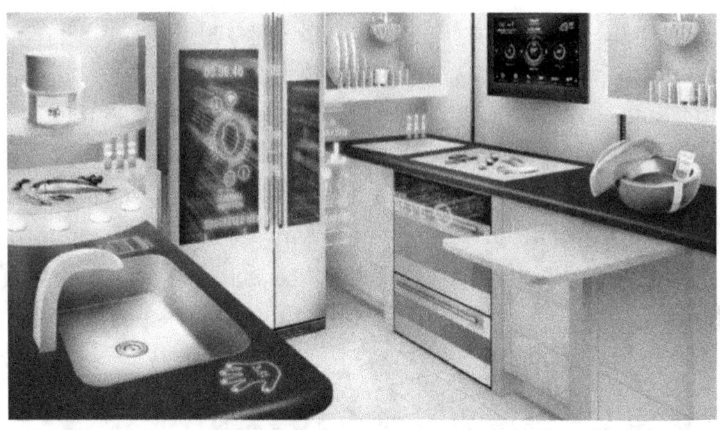

Sahil continued, "Now that we have come across VR, let me show you how it is used in future:-

VR was used in military training, so that soldiers can learn without any damage, as VR enables them to imitate the same area and weapons of war, but they are not real. Soldiers started training with the help of VR from 2050 onwards as seen in the hologram:-"

Sahil continued, "VR from the 22nd century was extensively used in healthcare, as it helps doctors to determine the disease and the best diagnosis of it. Doctors can see a magnified and clear image of an organ and can try their surgeries on that hologram created by VR, before enacting that on patients, to check their result. It can be seen in the hologram:-"

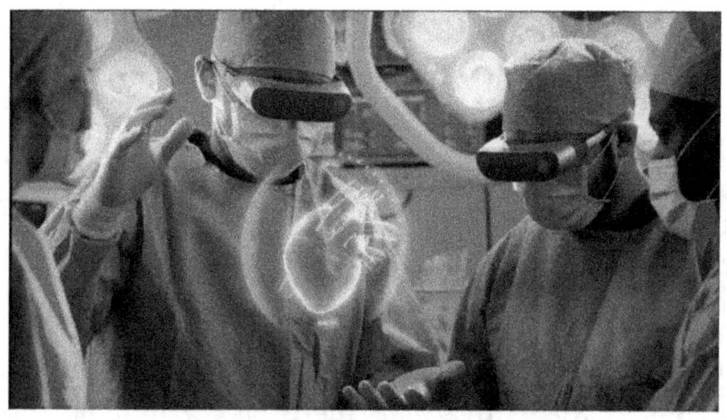

Sahil continued,"Even from the late 21st century, VR started changing the education sector and made studies very easy and interesting. See that in hologram:-"

Sahil said,"This way VR(Virtual Reality) shaped the future." Finally he took a break.

I was astonished by watching such realms of technology. When asked by Sahil, "How was it?". I replied, "Its Beauty can't be expressed in words."

I questioned out of curiosity, "If everything is so beautiful about the future then how did the world war start?"

Sahil looked at me as if I had asked something unpleasant. His face started showing some signs of despair. He finally started, "As you have seen, till now, the future was really very bright. Humanity progressed a lot until the mid- 22nd century. We developed new technologies, built new businesses, increased our satisfaction and happiness level. Even till 2050, there was a tremendous rise in creative fields, but thereafter things started changing." Sahil sighed. "The world was best till 2150, but then the clouds of grief and greed started overshadowing the sky. In the 22nd century, a new and creative field was Artificial Intelligence which was aimed to transform the world to a completely new place, to perform various tasks with humans. By the way, do you know the meaning of A.I.?"

I answered, "Yes, I think I have heard this term. It means programs which can do various tasks like humans and even learn from their mistakes just like humans."

Sahil continued,"Yeah, you are perfectly right. As believed in early 21st century, **Artificial Intelligence (A.I.)** will do those tasks which are considered monotonous, boring and simple. This way humans can focus on more complex works. In the development period of A.I., it only did easy and monotonous tasks, like those at call centres, recording day to day business transactions, etc. But a breakthrough came in the 2150s, where humans learnt to develop extremely complex programs." Here is its look:-

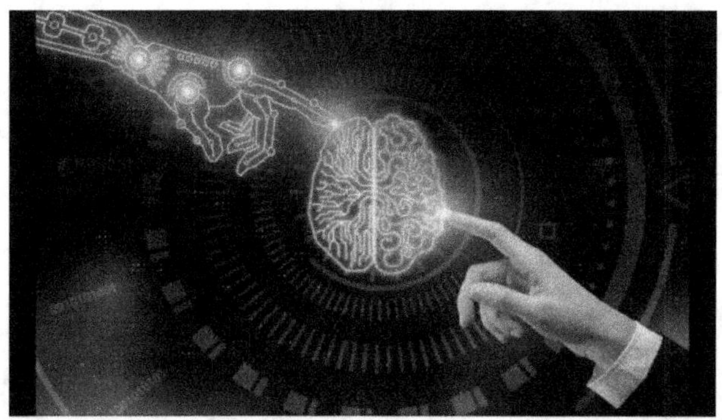

Mary was coming and listening to what Sahil said, she continued,"Ohh, so you are talking about the dark side of the future. Whenever I think of it, I get overwhelmed with negative emotions but Leo must learn the complete facts." Mary sat down beside Sahil and continued, "so, now let me take the topic further. As Sahil said, In the 21st century, various simple A.I. programs were built which helped humans in development. When all the monotonous tasks were done by A.I., we worked hand-in-hand to make the world a better place. AI created various types of employment which again we can't share otherwise it will change the future, but as believed AI helped greatly to build a bright future. But in the 22nd century things started changing. Humans have now developed intellect and vision to build AI which can perform complex tasks."

I said, "I have seen these types of theories in movies from my time. So, is it that AI has taken control of humans and we are fighting against machines? Why do humans have not taken proper steps to control the development of AI?"

Mary chuckled, "No, we are not fighting a war against AI, as interesting as that might sound. We developed and made complex programs but still not so complex that they can outperform our intellect. And when you talk about development, with increase in knowledge, no one in the early 22nd century bothered to think of what harm can complex programs do, they were with the vision that if all works are done by programs then we are free to enjoy our life. But it didn't happen that way..."

Sahil continued, "AI slowly took over all sectors. And when they were self-reliant enough to make proper decisions, they were even introduced in the judiciary," Sahil looked quite pensive as he traced the rim of his coffee mug. "Although many might argue against it, I firmly believe that was the start of what doomed future we are up against."

At my questioning look he chuckled. He said, "Yeah, I believe my explanation was rather brief. Let me elaborate. You know there are lawyers who study various court cases, laws, verdicts, etc. in their education. Then with the help of this knowledge they fight cases and save their clients. Similarly, AI bots were programmed with tons of legal information in the late 22nd century, so that they can fight cases and save their clients. AI bots started performing much better than human lawyers as they can store more information, they can think of various possibilities of winning cases, and they can predict the judgement beforehand. This way people started preferring AI law bots to lawyers. And till half of the 23rd century, most lawyers were subjected to unemployment."

Sahil continued, "Well.... now that the AI was proven to have as much reliability in making decisions as any human being, they were put into other departments as well."

Mary took over, "Now just as lawyers, they snatched employment of doctors as well. In the initial years of the 23rd century, such AI bots were made which can perfectly examine a human body for various diseases like brain tumour, cancer, heart issues, etc. They can also perform complex surgeries and operations. Everyone preferred these bots for they could not make mistakes in a diagnosis, they were more efficient in surgeries and operations, and they had more knowledge than real doctors. This way most doctors became unemployed by 2350. They had all the data just fit in them, so there was little room for error. They were scattered everywhere, they recorded everything. And they even took over the journalism department as well. Because with IOT devices connected, AI displayed everyone news of their interest accordingly in voice and virtual manner. So there was no need for journalists thereafter. You get the idea don't you?" I nodded.

Sahil continued, "Mechanical and automobile engineers too got unemployed in the 23rd century as AI programs were built which can design, test, and build cars and machines. They learn from their mistakes and improve further. Why would anyone employ people when AI did the same job at a cheaper cost more efficiently? Therefore, massive unemployment was seen in each and every sector by the 2350s."

I bit my lip, finally understanding the situation, "Then... you mean no one could find jobs, all sectors were overtaken by AI?"

Mary started, "Yes, the only ones with jobs were the ones highly skilled in a particular area. As we said, lawyers got unemployed because of LAW AI programs. You must be wondering who makes these AI programs.... well, the world's best lawyers are the ones who are also mastered in AI that are tasked with this. Similarly, in every sector, World's best skilled people programmed AI bots for their sector. Therefore, every individual from the late 21st century studies not only their profession but also AI. Every individual tried to be the best in their area, otherwise their worth would be zero. In the financial sector, Financial masterminds programmed Financial AI bots. In medicine, World's best doctors programmed Medical AI bots. Similarly in the education sector, World's best teachers programmed Mentor AI bots".

Sahil continued, "This way, every individual mastered AI with their profession. Apart from them those were employed who had expertise in multiple areas. Like a doctor who had also studied law. These individuals created a new organization called 'Mixed Talents' where they merged different professions into one and created an entirely new one like... Ohh I don't think we can tell you much about MIXED TALENT individuals as it can change the future if 21st century people know how to develop and get employment on the basis of multiple talents. You can say that these individuals found new opportunities and contributed in the development of the world."

"Mariana! Do you realize what you have done?" I flinched at the aggressive voice that filled the room. I looked at the entrance to see a dark skinned man with dark hair who seemed to be in his late fifties standing there with his face twisted with fury.

"C-commander! What happened?" Mary stuttered as the bulky man approached her.

"Follow me," his voice was commanding and left little room to argue. Sahil and I dashed after them as the commander dragged Mary to what seemed like the uppermost floor of the time machine.

We walked through what seemed like a prison with electric walls instead of bars. "This is the isolation ward." Sahil explained. "We keep intruders and minds invaded here."

"Mind invaded?" I wondered aloud.

"Later," Sahil said. They stopped in front of a cell where the electric wall had been deactivated. In there was nothing, but a pile of ashes sprawled across the floor. I watched as Mary's eyes darkened at the sight. "Is that Delucia's cell?" Sahil asked, his eyes wide with horror.

The commander huffed and they took it as a yes. "No, this...this can't be.... my calculations were perfect. What could have went wrong?" Mary mumbled, as horror took over her expression.

I watched as she fell down to her knees in despair and how Sahil went to comfort her.

"We have already lost so many of our own because of those crazy old bastards and because of you we have lost another," the commander's words were filled with emotion and I could tell that he cared deeply for those who worked under him.

"You must be punished for this Mariana. You will be tied in Cider for ten hours and you have to face electric shocks."

"Commander!" Sahil protested.

"What's Cider?" I whispered to Sahil who stood beside me. Sahil said, "It's the cell where severe punishments are given to the wrong doers."

"My commands shall be obeyed. Mary's blunder cost the life of a comrade."

"It... it was my fault," Mary mumbled. "I have to suffer the consequences. I was the one tasked with making the protonic shock gun. And it was my fault that Delucia..." Mary choked on a sob.

.... was it the one that Akito had come to claim... and the one that was kept right outside Mary's lab. If it was....

I looked at Mary's despair stricken face, then at the Commander, whose eyes were filled with tears but his heart was hard as stone.

I couldn't see Mary in despair. Mary would never tell but this mistake happened because of me. I distracted Mary from het work. I wasted her time to quench my curiosity of the future. I have to help Mary. I knew that Mary could never be mine but I wanted her to be filled with happiness, I couldn't see her in pain. I wanted to take all her pain and face them myself. I clenched a fist and resolved myself to take on the consequences of my decision.

With tears in my eyes and a sore throat, I announced "I want to say something Commander. You are making a wrong decision. It wasn't Mary's fault. It was ..... mine." My words were stuck in my mouth as I saw Mary crying and tears streamed down her eyes.

CHAPTER 5
MYSTERIES OF WAR UNRAVELLED

I couldn't help but flinch when the commander stared at me with eyes full of resentment. I could feel that he was deeply concerned about something, even though I couldn't make heads or tails of the situation.

"If this is about the weapon from earlier, the one Akito came to take... well, you know when that alarm went off earlier? I kind of bumped into it when I rushed out of Mary's lab. When I tried to place it back, I might have set something... off." I looked away, unable to meet Mary's eyes. Although it was a lie to protect her, the best lie was one even your allies would believe.

While I was fiddling with the hem of my shirt, I didn't notice the commander walking right up to me until he was inches away. He grabbed my collar and pushed his forehead against mine. "You... I've never seen you before. Who are you?"

"I am from 2021, and I...."

"Oh. You are that child," the commander massaged his temples and let out a strained groin. "Look, I know it was our fault that you traveled through time with us, but you can't go messing around with sensitive equipment. You will be taking the punishment I announced for Mariana. Sahil! See to it that he learns his lesson."

"But commander-" Sahil said in order to defend me.

"Not another word," he ordered before he strode off. I looked at Sahil and then at Mary, who was still sitting on the ground and was now looking at me as if horror stricken.

She pushed herself up and grabbed my collar. "You lied. Didn't you? I know I was not with you when the alarm went off, but I know the weapon was just as I had left it."

I gave her a sad smile, as tears welled up in her eyes. "Well. It was a white lie, I suppose. At least you won't suffer," I said.

"You are such an idiot!" Although she yelled that, she pulled me into a tight hug. "You don't have to do this for me. It was my fault after all. I should have tested it out before handing it over. I am sorry you have to..."

"Hey, don't say that. From what I've heard, you must be in some turbulent times. It's normal to make mistakes when you are under a lot of stress. Besides, you had to take care of me all day. You didn't have time to test it out."

"Mary!" Mary pulled out from our hug as Sahil placed a hand on her shoulder. "You should go back for now. We can't defy the commander. I have to take him..."

I saw Sahil's eyes darken from the thought of putting me through electric shocks, but despite that I was glad it was me and not Mary. Even the thought of being electrocuted, terrified me, but I kept telling myself. "It's for Mary."

I gave Mary a nod, assuring her that there was not much to worry about and followed Sahil.

Sahil showed me to a room, it was just like a prison cell. Outside on the wall was a button-like device. The cell was covered with transparent electric walls. Sahil pressed that button like device and switched off the walls and let me in the cell; then he bound me by what looked like ropes made of metal, and fixed me in a round machine and walked to the other end of the room. His eyes met mine and I could see that they were swollen from holding back tears. Along with Sahil, there were few men outside the cell, holding electric guns, as this cell was made for the punishment of evil people.

"So... before we start, I will explain to you what exactly your punishment is." His voice strained and I could feel that it wasn't any for him to inflict pain on someone as it was for me to suffer it.

"This switch here, as you can see, when I flip it on, electricity will pass through those ropes to you. These shocks are controlled, you will not die but..... the pain you are about to experience is like 10 snakes biting you at the same time." Tears started appearing in his eyes. "I will flip the switch on in exactly five seconds. Brace yourself." I gulped at the thought of electricity running through my skin and shuddered from the thought. But to Sahil, I gave him a nod. He counted down to five and as he finally said zero and flipped on the switch, I couldn't help but let out a scream at the sudden pain that covered my entire body.

It was extremely, extremely painful. "Say," Sahil asked after a few minutes. "It hasn't even been a day since you arrived. How can you take on something like this for Mary? Is it even natural to be that.... I can't even think of a word...."

"In love?"

"I was going to say stupid, but let's go with that," Sahil said.

"Well... argh... I love her. I can sacrifice anything for her happiness," I said in between moans.

"Are you sure you are not just a masochist?"

"Of course not!" I yelled.

Sahil gave me a chuckle. "You are an idiot. But I can't deny it. You are a good guy. I am even willing to allow Mary to date you. Congratulations on earning Sahil's approval. Let me tell you, it's not that easy to procure."

Despite my pain, I couldn't help but chuckle.

After another few minutes of silence, to forget my pain I asked, "This war... what exactly is it about?"

Sahil was silent for a moment, I almost thought that he hadn't heard my question when he said it.

"Honestly, I am not so sure myself. Much like everything else, it's something passed down to us by our predecessors. It is basically a race against time. Everyone is looking for the same thing. A bomb that can end the universe."

"The... universe? Not just a specific location?" Sahil shook his head and looked at me with sad eyes.

"The ones that are participating in this war are divided into fractions. URJA (Our group) and the Revolution Seekers. We are Urja. The revolution seekers intend to detonate the bomb and end the universe."

"But... why?"

"They want to recreate the world. They think if they end the world by detonating that bomb, they can prevent the end of humanity."

"That's.... messed up. That doesn't make any sense." I said before letting out another grunt from the pain.

"Honestly, I don't understand much about their ideals either. But... that's who we are fighting." Sahil sighed. "And they've got pretty big powerhouses on their side."

"Powerhouses?"

"Well... URJA is a group with a majority of relatively younger people. And the Revolution Seekers... they are like old people with so much more experience and knowledge and then there's him." He said almost sounding disgusted.

"Him?" I asked.

"The thinker. That's what we call him. He's a genius. His real name is confidential, but what we do know is that he has the insight akin to the sharpest minds history had ever seen. He can predict anything outside and inside the battlefield like he has seen the future."

"If time machines are available, is that really that amazing?"

"Traveling to the future is much more dangerous than traveling to the past. It can literally rip your limbs off. Not many people are brave or stupid enough to attempt that. Especially not him. Although his predictions and strategies are spot on, he is a total coward. No one has ever seen him out in the open. he's a commander who has never seen the battle field," Sahil explained.

"There's one other thing I was curious about," I had gotten used to the electricity running in my body, and my grunts of pain weren't as frequent as before.

"Ask away."

"The commander.... he seemed terribly concerned about something. What could that be?"

Sahil looked at me. "I am impressed you have the insight to notice that."

Sahil shrugged. "You see, even though the two factions are openly hostile toward each other, we haven't exactly done open fire at each other. The state remains somewhat akin to a cold war. We are developing weapons. We are sending spies to each other. You get the idea. But.... Now that Mary's weapon has killed a couple of them, they might see this as a chance to declare actual war on us. Real battle is not that far away, I'm afraid."

"If a war is what they wanted, what stopped them for so long."

Sahil looked at me as if I had asked a dumb question. "Well... even at times like this, we need resources. And that we usually get from traders who are not a part of either faction. We won't be able to develop anything without their support. But, you know... war is poison to society. The common public would hate it. So whoever declared war first, would lose the support of the public and be isolated from most resources. And now that two of them were killed here, nothing's stopping them from it."

"But I thought the war was about finding the bomb," I asked, confused.

"Well.... we don't know who yet... but someone spread false information that we found it."

"What? Why would anyone do that?"

"Like I said, we don't know." Sahil uttered
"But-"
"Sahil! Time's up. We can release him now."

I sighed at Akito's entrance. The pain was finally over. "Everyone has to gather in the main hall. Commander said to bring him along."

Sahil flipped off the switch and freed me from my bindings. I shook my whole body to calm down the jitters and get rid of the goosebumps before following the other two to the mess hall.

Most of the people that lived in the time machine had gathered there, so it was pretty crowded. The commander, along with Jessie were standing on a makeshift stage. The commander, in contrast to Jessie's pale skin, had very dark skin and his clothes were black as well. With serious expression as he gazed down at the crowd, he looked pretty darn intimidating.

"Now that everyone is here, I should start," the commander said, his voice daunting. "I'm afraid they will come upon us soon." The room filled with gasps and whispers.

"Silence!" He yelled. He looked around in the crowd and his eyes settled on me. "Unfortunately, due to a mistake two of the Revolution Seekers met their end." Gasps filled the room yet again.

"Because of this, they might make their move rather soon. I believe we should expect an attack as soon as next week." The whispers and fear were slowly getting out of control. "For the new recruits who came from civilian camps not too long ago and our little uninvited guest from the twenty first century, I shall explain the situation once more." He turned to Jessie. The twenty two year old gave him a nod and moved to bring out what looked like a hybrid between a pen drive and a search light. She inserted it on a socket on the podium and a hologram showed up.

It showed what looked like a ball of blue light and a thin translucent green layer covered it. Satellites were circling around it like. I could see cubical devices connected with thin wires wrapped around the green layer in a circle. It was like a part of a dark universe with some lights.

"This energy you see here is present in the Andromeda galaxy, billions of light years away. It was accidentally discovered by Dr. Vikram in the late twenty first century. Dr. Vikram, a man who changed the society, nation and world to a harmonious place. He was the most successful entrepreneur till date, and his businesses served various missions which were extremely important for humanity. He served the poor, educated children, and did research in economics, physics and space. He also made discoveries and established businesses to improve the years of life. He himself lived 158 years, and has done various things for which the world will remember him forever. Once in his space research, he found this energy billions of light years away and made a company to study it if it can be used for the betterment of the world. When his space research high speed rays reached near this energy, it got reflected by a green barrier which was completely opaque. But through years of tinkering, Dr. Vikram was able to destroy the barrier, so as to study the energy in depth. Then he sent his satellites inside it after immediately destroying the barrier, but he lost connection to it immediately. Many satellites were sent and when the barrier was demolished, he figured out that the energy inside the barrier had destroyed the satellites. No... that is too mild a term. It completely disappeared, neither scrapes nor ashes remained."

I gulped, "How can something do that? Destroying matter... is that even possible?"

"When Dr. Vikram realized how catastrophic this energy was, he immediately halted his research on it and decided to make another barrier which can stop this energy. After some more studying, he found that what seems like energy is not even energy, it was **Antimatter**."

"But what's Antimatter?", a teenager from our crew asked.

Commander explained to everyone, "Antimatter is something which is just like matter but has opposite charges. If matter collides with antimatter then it results in the production of energy but matter and antimatter both disappear. It's just like a chemical reaction but *if that anti-matter wave gets in motion and enters our Universe made of matter then we all will vanish, and just energy will remain.* Therefore, Dr. Vikram Bhatt made an artificial barrier, to stop the anti-matter from coming into our Universe and placed it at the exact same place, as you can see in this hologram. "

The Commander continued, "Dr. Vikram was a visionary man. He knew that the world is continually developing and there are various productive uses of antimatter. So he thought that if in the future, the generation found a way to stop anti-matter and to make something worthy and productive of it, then they must be accessible to this antimatter. Therefore, he made the barrier removable but the removing mechanism is not simple at all. He made an IOT briefcase, (which is made with such compounds as it can withstand any temperature, energy ,etc. It can't be destroyed even by a nuclear bomb and can be put anywhere including space), in which there exists a small button which if pressed will set the destruction of the artificial barrier and will start the motion of the anti-matter wave, but that suitcase is locked and opens by a voice-password which no one knows. For better security, Dr. Vikram passed on this briefcase to his next generation just before his death and his next generation hid the briefcase in some part of the universe." He said pointing to the wire connection cubes. "There is an Enter option, which if pressed will start programs for reversing the barrier and will eventually remove the energy barrier. No one knows where the Briefcase is. But that's what we, as well as the ReS (Revolution Seekers) have been searching for all these years [From 2305 to 2340]."

I stared at the ball of energy and a shiver ran down my spine at the thought of something so destructive setting loose in the universe.

Jessie took over from the commander and showed a new hologram and continued, "By 2250, AI had completely taken over the majority of the sectors, and there was little need for humane employees, therefore Dreamscape was introduced. As most of you know, because of A.I just the best people of a certain sector which programmed those bots or the people with mixed talents were able to find paid jobs. But those who were average in intellect, those who just had creative talents, they all were left with no work. The economy was built in such a way that the one who works is the one who earns. As these people didn't have work, they had to suffer from poverty, hunger and diseases. Those intelligent minds got extremely wealthy, they started owning countries and these less intelligent people (constituting 95% of population) had to suffer. The intelligent people finally took this issue in light. They had various discussions on what to do with this poor population. There was a world summit of best intellects in the 2270s and they discussed solutions to this problem. One solution came as they all should be killed as they are just exploiting world resources and are of no use now to the world. But even among intellectuals, there were few people who discarded this idea, saying everyone should live their life. After some months of discussion, finally everyone agreed on the idea of dreamscape."

The Commander continued, "Dreamscape was initially built for recreation, but in 2230s, it became a mind controlling machine which gets connected to your brain and will bring you in a state of deep sleep wherein can imagine the best time of your life, your childhood, time with your friends and family, and so many more beautiful memories, you can live them in dreams but they will be same as reality to you. It was revolutionary and many people took this machine to their homes and used it at night to get dissolved in their happy memories. But the Great Intellects planned to use it soon as a device to solve economic problems. They decided that unemployed people (95% of population) had nothing more to contribute to their nations and society, since these Great Minds along with AI could now manage the world. So these unemployed people could be sent to their dreams with the help of these machines and get in deep sleep with happy memories for lifetime,here they will be alive not dead. They can actually live their complete lives in peaceful dreams and after 70 to 100 years, after which they will automatically die and will get out of their happy dreams. Intellectuals said that this would even be beneficial for the world as when a person is happy, he emits lots of energy. Therefore, though these people will be in dreams but as they will be happy, they will emit a myriad of energies which can be utilised in various purposes of development. This can create heaven on earth for everyone, according to Great minds. This can be seen in the hologram, where kids, men, women, all were kept in cocoon-like structures made of A.I. programs to take their energies and keep them in dreams."

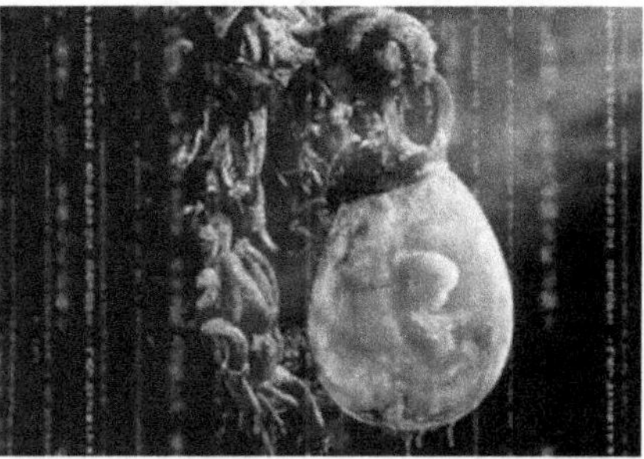

Jessie continued, "But this wasn't right. In the 2290s this plan was started and by the end of the 23rd century, it was almost completed. People thought that from the 24th century, earth will be heaven but various intelligents started getting greedy and ambitious for power. Various intellectuals thought that now they can conquer our world and thereby conquer the entire Universe, controlling it in their way. This group became known as the Revolution seekers who were in search of the briefcase made by Dr. Vikram as mentioned above. They have theories that if they remove the barrier, anti-matter will destroy the complete Universe of matter, but not them. We are not even able to predict how they are saying this, as according to us, everyone will die if that massacre happens."

I looked at the commander's strained eyebrows. "The Revolution Seekers have influence among other intellectuals and they hide their ulterior motives by saying they want to create a new world. They say that they aim to restart the complete Universe in a more profound way in which there is no poverty, no illiteracy, no sufferings. But we, URJA, know that they want to just control the Universe and therefore we aim to rebuild the world, the way it is by countering their highly idealistic and optimistic view."

The commander sighed with exasperation. Jessie continued for him, "someone has been spreading rumors, rumors that we have found the trigger for that bomb, even though it's not true. ReS have been looking for a reason to attack our base and unfortunately, they have found it. We should expect a full scale attack any time now."

Murmurs broke out in the room. Cries of confidence in their attack force. Sobs of fear, whispers of consolement and screams of defiance spread throughout the mess hall.

I could feel the fear of an attack run all over my being. All the hair on my limbs were as straight as trees, my palms were shivering with terror, my teeth were chattering. I clamped my hands together to stop them from shivering, but it was of no use. I turned to see Sahil place a consoling hand on my shoulder. He gave me a sad smile and turned to the stage once again.

I saw Jessie started giving orders to her subordinates and the noncombatant staff slowly receding to their labs. I was about to leave when I caught the commander looking in my direction. I told Sahil to wait for me and walked up to the commander.

"Child," he said as he scanned me. "I hope there are no serious injuries from your punishment?" I shook my head at his question. The commander gave me a nod and beckoned me to sit on the stage with him.

"I hope you don't take this the wrong way. I don't wish any harm upon anyone." His eyes turned wet with tears.

"I understand. You had to punish me. After all, I did make a huge mistake," I said. "I literally caused a war to break out."

"And that shall weigh heavily upon us. But I should have gone against my rules, this time as you are here because of our mistake. I'm sorry for it."

"No please don't apologise at all. I was even thinking, can I be a part of your team and fight for the survival of humanity? I can recall that in my time, I was a very good sportsman and gymnast."

Commander was pleased, "Amazing son. You are brave and compassionate. I like you, my boy and I will surely look forward to it."

I asked,"Sir is our group as strong as theirs?"

"Yeah... the thing is... the people on their side are recognized individuals, they are famous and look reliable. On the other hand, a majority of URJA's members are... on the younger side. They are not very experienced and the public perceive us as a rebellious group of teenagers who think they can save the world." he sighed.

I could see how that could be a problem. Most people think of teenagers as an immature bunch who act on whims and refuse to take responsibility.

"I don't know about those ReS members, but I care about the people of URJA and if anything comes in their way of survival, I will destroy it, whether human or alien." I could see the fire in his eyes. A passion to protect those important to him. I could understand that. After all, I felt the same way about Mary and even Sahil. I wondered how I had become so attached to them, even though it had barely been a day and a half since I came here.

A day and a half. It felt like an eternity had already passed with all that happened. I couldn't hold in the yawn that escaped me. The commander patted my back and said, "with all that has conspired since you stumbled upon the time machine, I assume you are very tired. You should get some sleep before we the ReS catch wind of the death of their comrades and attack us." I gave the commander a nod and started to head toward Sahil.

~~~

What Leo didn't know was that Mary and Jessie were talking right across the hallway. He was not here to listen to this conversation.

"It really was my fault, but... but he took the blame for it." Mary said, her eyes were shut and she was biting her lip with anxiety as she leant against the wall with her arms crossed.
~~~

Jessie was standing right beside her, a weapon strung across her back as she listened to her friend. "He's too kind for his own good. How could he do this for me? We barely know each other," she mumbled.

"I get it. He is kind of an anomaly. Not many people can be that.... I don't even have a word for it. Do you think he might like you?"

Mary blushed. "I... I don't know. Do you think it's possible?" Jessie chuckled.

"Don't tell me you like him?" She teased.

Mary started fiddling with her fingers as her cheeks turned bright pink. "Maybe...? He did go through hours of electrocution for me. He has a very compassionate heart for which I was looking in every individual to find my partner but till now, I haven't found one. Of course I like him. Do you think he really likes me too?"
Jessie ruffled Mary's hair and pulled her into a hug. "You adorable little girl. Who wouldn't like you?" Mary with starry eyes embraced Jessie and hid herself in her shoulder to hide her embarrassment.

CHAPTER 6

WHERE IS DR. VIKRAM'S BRIEFCASE?

Trillions of light years away from the URJA timeship, a lone battleship was afloat in the Black eye galaxy. In the centre of the battleship, amidst a room filled with computer and holographic screens sat a man who looked in his late thirties.

The man sat on a magnetic IOT chair floating in air with the help of magnetism.

A young man stood in the room, he had just finished giving his report. "You may go," the man floating said to the young man.

"What idiocy. How could they trust a young girl with such sensitive equipment and allow a teenager from the 21st century to interfere with it?" A female voice said.

The man chuckled. "Oh, dear, how could you not understand? You are a brilliant strategist, and wife of the smartest man in the Universe. You should have known that child from the twenty first century had never even touched the gun, it was one of my men who had... tinkered with it."

"But our men died because of it." She spoke angrily.

He laced his fingers and said, "an inevitable sacrifice, for our greater good, for achieving our great objective of making a better world"

"I see. It seems even now I can't quite get into your head, my life partner as well as my most trusted comrade. Sorry, I got angry with you, I know Thinker has made the complete plan and he is never wrong" the woman staring at Thinker said, "You still look so beautiful as if you are still a little more than thirty."

Thinker said lovingly, "Same with you, credit goes to Dr. Vikram's medicine because of which highly qualified professionals are able to live for many years and still look young. Who can say that we are each in 130s? We have devoted our complete life to attain our objective and now I have planned everything and we are very close to achieving it."

The Thinker's wife says, " After we explode the Universe bomb, our group members will not be dead unlike everybody else but how will it happen, as no one knows this truth except you, my love?"

Thinker says, "That is something no-one should know except me. But after the end of Universe we will make a World where every individual will be as smart as us, free from human emotions which reduces one's potential. They will work for the development and Harmony of our society unlike our emotional and so less intellect counterpart Humans. We will achieve the target together."

Thinker's wife, "Yes my love. We will surely achieve it."

With a snicker, he asked. "So, what about the hypnotized URJA members. Are my little pets doing a good job?"

With a devilish smile, the woman said, "Indeed, we can expect results as soon as tomorrow."

~~~

Back to Time-machine of Urja
~~~

Leo thinks, Since we could travel in time and spent all hours in a wormhole, night and day were pretty hard to distinguish. So they had allotted sleeping hours, where everyone could rest and not lose their sanity.

I was in a narrow room with one bed, and one desk. And I stared at the metallic ceiling, wide awake. It was hard to lull myself to sleep after all the information fed to me in a single day. And the after effects of the pain from the electrocution were still ringing in my ear and the hair on my limbs were as sharp as needles from being charged, even though almost four days had passed.

I had been watching old recordings of Dr. Vikram's speeches and going through many of his digitized notes. Despite the fact that I had been working all the time. I couldn't get myself to sleep.

Giving up on getting any rest tonight, I decided to wander around in the time machine. As I walked toward the farm (a duplicate in a time-machine), I saw three people heading my way. Two boys, and an older woman. They seemed deep in conversation. I gave them a nod as a greeting, but they completely ignored me. I saw something bulging out from the coat of one of the boys. As my gaze lingered longer than I had intended, the boy turned around, his hands covering the bulging object.

With an awkward apology, I started walking away. Deviating from my original destination, I headed to Mary's lab. Although she was asleep, I remembered that I could order food from the menu, and I was itching for a late night snack.

As I reached the lab, I saw that the door to the lab was ajar. Was Mary in there?

At the sound of sparkling electricity, I almost jumped a mile. Though terrified, I looked for the source of the sound and saw the password lock on the lab's door. It was a mess. Wires were hanging out from everywhere and I could see the number buttons on the floor. I rushed in to see what was going on. The lab too was a complete mess. Everything was either smashed on the floor or had been crushed by something heavy.

Remembering the three from earlier, I fell into a panic. What did they steal? Could they... could they be trying to kill someone? But who? The commander?

As terrifying thoughts filled my head, I rushed to what I remembered to be Mary's room. After two minutes of impatient knocking, Mary finally opened the door. I watched as she rubbed off sleep from her eyes. I couldn't even take in her beauty despite the drowsiness. It was an urgent matter after all.

"I think the commander is in danger," I blurted out.

Mary's eyes widened and she grabbed what looked like a high tech gun and started leading me toward the commander's room.

"I ran into these three people who were acting incredibly suspicious." I explained as we ran, "they had completely trashed your lab and possibly even stolen some equipment."

"My lab?" Mary asked, she seemed disturbed by the fact that someone had gone through her lab.

When we reached the commander's room we saw that the boys had pinned the commander to the floor and the woman had Mary's gun pointed at him. I recognized it to be the gun that had killed those members of ReS. The one Mary had made a mistake while making and that obliterated people.

"I hope you have fixed whatever the problem was..."

Mary shook her head, "I didn't have the time." Mary pulled out the gun she had brought and shot the woman. She immediately collapsed. I saw a dart sticking out of the back of her neck.

"Tranquilizers." Mary explained before shooting the two boys as well. Although she managed to hit one of them despite their struggles she missed the second one. He launched herself at Mary. He was a well built guy, he could over power Mary easily. If he got to her, he might kill her without a second's hesitation. I looked at the terror building up in Mary's eyes as she fired darts in his direction, but missed her target in her terrified state. It was obvious that she could be knocked out by a single punch from him and so, to protect her, I launched myself at him, without a second thought. Pinning him down to the floor, it gave Mary the time to recover and shoot another dart at him.

I looked at the three people lying on the floor. The commander stood up, somewhat disoriented, he grabbed the wall for support. "You saved my life." He said.

I shrugged as I got up and dusted off my clothes. "It was no big deal."

"So... how did they breach your defenses?" I asked, looking down at the boy who had gone down last.

"They are our own people."

"What? You mean they betrayed you?"

Mary shook her head. "They were hypnotized. ReS has developed a device that can send waves to the brain and mess with it so you think that you are doing something you want, but are actually doing the opposite. We call the victims of this device the 'mind invaded'. You saw the cells downstairs, they are used to contain these people. After a few hours, the hypnotiser effect gets over and then they become our normal comrades."

I turned to the sound of footsteps and noticed more than a few people heading our way. Sahil was one of them. As they approached Mary, she explained, "Mind invaded."

Sahil looked at them and his eyes widened. "Shelby and her sons? I was teaching them combat lessons only until yesterday." He sighed as others moved to take the three to the below deck cells.

Mary and I took turns to explain what had happened to Sahil. "Huh? I guess some good came of that electrocution after all." He chuckled.

"Yeah... I guess-"

"You are bleeding!" Mary yelled. I turned to see blood gushing out of my right arm.

"The guy must have grazed it somehow." I mumbled as I pressed my palm against my wound to stop the bleeding.

Mary grabbed the hem of my top and started to pull me. "We are going to the infirmary."

"You go ahead and I'll be there in a second."

I clenched my fist at the stinging pain as Mary wiped off the blood from a cotton ball. She strangely had some tears in her eyes. I asked, "Why are you crying."

She said, "Nothing.... Just Don't you ever do that again."

"Do what?"

Mary rolled her eyes and said, "Idiot. Don't start jumping in front of hostile people like that. This time it was just a wound, next time it could be much more serious." Her eyes had a very serious gloomy look.

"But he could have hurt you."

"My safety is my concern. You don't have to hurt yourself for me." She said as she started to clean up the counter that was littered with medicines and gauze.

"If it means you are out of harm's way, I wouldn't care if it even kills me. I... care for you."

She said, "But why.... Why so much care for me, why so much affection for me?"

My heartbeat increased, I said, " I don't know.. whenever you get hurt, it hurts me... Whenever you are happy, it jocunds me.... I can withstand all pain but can't see you in pain."

Mary with a very loving smile said, "Do you love me...?"

I hesitated, " Ummmm.... But how does it matter.. You love Akito and he loves you and you make up the best couple. I have no right to come in between."

I saw Mary's hands paused before she turned to look at me. "Who said I like Akito?"

"Well. You got along really well. And.. he is so handsome and perfect and..."

My eyes widened when Mary pressed her lips to mine. She kissed me! Mary pulled out and looked me straight in my eye. "Akito and I grew up together, he is my childhood friend. That's all there is to it. I always need someone who can understand me completely, who can sacrifice everything for me, who loves me purely not for my looks but for my heart and you are perfect for it but I'm not perfect."

I stopped her right there, "Never say that again... You are absolutely perfect."

She smiled, "I have various shortcomings as you have seen in my weapon development. I make mistakes and I'm not as compassionate as you."

I said, "We will together overcome all our shortcomings and will have a bright and happy future. I love you"

My eyes almost filled with tears. "I love you," she responded back. Before I could even think to control myself, I slipped my hand into her hair and kissed her. And she kissed back. I took in the scent of grease and metal covering her. But that's who she was, an expert on making and reverse engineering weapons. Her hair was softer than cotton, her lips as smooth as silk. Mary grabbed my shoulder and then slid her hands to wrap around my head. Euphoria. I finally understood that feeling.

She treated my wound and gave me some pills and I downed it with some water. I felt the pain go away and my wound healed in an instant leaving nothing but a white scar. I looked at Mary, my eyes wide open. After a short chuckle, she said, "the medicine speeds up body function. Although it was a small dose, you will feel..." My stomach growled loudly and I blushed from embarrassment. Mary chuckled. "It speeds up all functions including digestion, so you might want to find a toilet and some food." I nodded my head.

At the sound of a cough we both pulled apart. "I see you two are getting along well." Sahil said. Both of ours cheeks turned red to his teasing. "The commander has called for an emergency meeting."

"Alright." Mary and I shared a glance and smiled at each other. I held her hand and together, we walked toward what would be a turning point in our lives.

When we reached the mess hall, everyone seemed to be in a state of panic. It seemed that news about the plot against the commander's life had spread like wildfire.

"Ever since the time machine was invented, time always worked for us, however, right now, it's working against us again. We are very short on time. We need to find the trigger immediately.1 before ReS gets a hand on it or declares a full scale war on us."

Unlike the last time, everyone seemed to be utterly silent. But the silence was fragile. I heard a sneeze from the other sound of the room. And as if a switch had been turned on, utter chaos spread throughout the mess. I saw as people completely broke down in cold sweat, some even fainted.

I looked at the commander. He too seemed very nervous.

"The commander brought out a loudspeaker and yelled for everyone to keep quiet. Being calm, even the commander couldn't expect us to be calm at this point."

"Although we refrained from doing so earlier, it seems that we have to split up our forces. Putting Jessie's combat platoon aside, we will be forming four groups to search for the trigger. Team one will consist of...."

The commander continued to assign names I did not know to the expeditions. Until, "... and Leo." It seemed that I had been assigned to group four. Akito was with me and he is assigned to be our group leader. He walked up to me and those assigned to our group followed along. Sahil was a member of Jessie's platoon, so he moved to her side and Mary, a member of the tech department, walked to what seemed like a gathering of the technicians.

"Hello my fellow comrades. Our job is to search for Dr. Vikram's Briefcase in various places, time-periods, etc. I have received our assigned timeline. We will be looking for the trigger in between various centuries. Pack your gear and essentials. We will be leaving in two hours," Akito said.

I watched the others disperse. Our group had ten members including me and Akito. As I followed Akito to his room.

He handed me a duffel bag. "I have to pack some emergency supplies. I hope you don't mind carrying some of my stuff."

"I don't mind," I said, looking around his room. It was neat and tidy and perfect. It was like no one even lived there. Even though Marianna and I confessed to each other, I was still a little jealous of his perfectness. Wait, is perfectness even an actual word?

Deciding to spend these few hours with Mary, I decided to go to her lab. I saw her chewing something and staring at what looked like the blueprints of a weapon. As she was immersed in it completely, she noticed differently when I sneaked up on her and hugged her from behind. "Leo?" She seemed surprised.

"What are you doing?" I asked. I put a smile on my face as she rambled on about developing weapons for the war.

"So what are you doing here?" She asked. "Our group will leave in..." I looked at my watch, "an hour and a half. Akito told me that no matter how much time we take it doesn't matter, but for you and the others on the time machine it would be about two weeks until we meet again. I was melancholic to go at such a time when we both have showed our love to each other. I wanted to be with her, talk with her but circumstances weren't in our favour.

I saw her eyes darken. "I won't see you and Akito for two weeks?" I shrugged and wrapped my arms around her. "I guess it can't be helped, huh."

We haven't shed tears as we know this separation is temporary and for a good purpose: Saving Humanity.

After two hours the ten of us assembled in a room at the far end of the time machine. I saw two cylindrical boxes with complex controls. "These are time capsules. When we need to travel through time in small groups, we use this instead of moving the entire time machine. It can accommodate upto five people," Akito explained to me. Then raising his voice a little, he addressed the group. "The coordinates and the time have already been set, Selena, you take charge of the second sub group."

"Yes sir." Then everyone settled in either time-capsule.

"So guys we will meet in a new time-line. All the best for your Journey." Akito uttered.

~~~

Our expedition started.

We first went to the sixteenth century in Shakespeare's time, we don't just have to search for the briefcase but we also have to keep in mind that the timeline is not to be altered because of us. One of our team's members suggested that as Shakespeare is one of the most renowned dramatists and Dr. Vikram admired him a lot, we may find some evidence from his time. We went to his home where he used to live with his Wife and Children. We then searched his drama stage and his various drama works for some evidence but we found nothing. During our search we were suddenly noticed by him and he greeted us.

He said something we don't fully understand but we used translators and kept them in our ears by which his complex language got translated to simple English. So he said, "Hello guys. You seem to be foreigners."

Akito greeted him and explained to him that we are in search of something. Shakespeare wished that we get the thing we desire. He came with us to a shop, where he asked for food grains. The Shopkeeper rejected his demand saying, "You have not still repaid your previous dues. I think you are the laziest person who just writes rubbish without doing any hard work."
~~~

Shakespeare tried to explain, "I'm doing something which will shape the society and make people more educated about emotions and philosophies of our life."

But the shopkeeper paid no heed to his explanation. We had some currency of that period and we paid on his behalf. He thanked us and asked the name of Akito.

Akito said, "I'm Bassanio, he lied just to prevent changes in timeline." The Bard of Avon said, "I will surely mention your name in one of my dramas, as a noble and compassionate person."

But we found nothing there, so finally we went to the era of industrial revolution and searched in that timeframe. Though we gained a lot of experience about how modern society evolved, we found nothing even there.

Then we went to the deepest point of the ocean. We saw various fishes, completely dark blueish water, and various marine creatures. This looked so amazing but proved to be of no use. I was really glad to experience such marvelous adventures.

We then went to the places of the first and second world wars. The sufferings of soldiers really touched our hearts. Death loomed everywhere, blood flowed more than water. We saw a soldier whose one hand was cut off from his body, he was walking with difficulty and his body was covered in blood. We helped him and gave him water. We urged him to go to the treatment faculty but he said he just has very little time left, he wants to use that to recall all the memories of his life with his parents, friends and wife. He thanked us, his eyes wet and advocated the sufferings he went through in his life. It even motivated us to do much hard work to stop the war of the 24th century from becoming like it.

This way we kept travelling and finally one day, we settled at a place and discussed our expeditions.

"We have already searched through the whole of the twentieth and previous centuries. Will we even find this thing?" Selena groaned.

"I know right. By leaping to every twenty years we have searched almost everywhere. Two months... or maybe even more have passed." I said as I rested my head on Akito's lap, while we were having lunch by a campfire. In these two months I had grown pretty close to Akito. Although I missed Mary, life wasn't all about romance. Friends were important as well. And I could swear to myself that my friendship with Akito was something I needed. A friend is a guy to tell everything to.

"You must really miss her, huh, Leo."

"Her? You mean, Mary?" I looked at Serena.

"Of course... I wish I could just run to her arms this instant." Serena giggled at my shameless proclamation.

"You really are something." She said shaking her head as if fed up with me.

"I bet you want to grow old together and then rest in peace with your Graves side by side, huh? But is that even possible? Considering you have to go back in time? Speaking of that... why don't we just leave you there? In your time I mean?" Selena said mockingly.

As Serena said that, I got up from my sleeping stance. Reality had hit hard. I had to go back to my time. My family was probably waiting for me. I wanted to stay with Mary but... whenever I thought about abandoning my past and my family an ache spread throughout my heart.

"We have to bring his memories back first," Akito said, looking at my troubled expression.

"Right."

"If you get your memories back, I believe your choice might be easier."

Or tougher, I thought. Then I would have to choose between Mary and a family I remembered. How could I ever make that choice?

Wait... "grave." I said,

"What?"

"Dr. Vikram's grave. We didn't check his grave, did we? As a person like Dr. Vikram will like to keep the precious creation of his life, which has such a dangerous impact on the human world, with himself even after his death. So, his grave may contain his Briefcase."

Our eyes widened at the same time and we rushed toward the time capsules. Within seconds we were in the twenty second century. Where lay the grave of Dr. Vikram who died at the age of 158.

"So we are gravediggers now, huh?" One of our group members said as he plunged the shovel into the dirt.

After a while, he stopped digging. Just on the coffin, lay a briefcase. Akito inspected it and said, "It is activated by a voice password."

"Let's get back to the time machine immediately. We will have the tech department deal with that." Selena said and we continued toward the time capsules.

~~~

(Inside Thinker's room)

"They found the trigger," the Thinker's wife said and looked at her husband impatiently.

"Don't worry, love. It is all a part of the master plan." Thinker said.

As he pressed a button, the hologram of a man showed up.

"Isn't that...?" His wife said in shock.

"All is according to plan, sir." A young man said.

The thinker laughed menacingly. "I don't know what I would have done without you, Sahil."
~~~

CHAPTER 7
THE APOCALYPSE

Mary, Akito, Sahil and I were sitting around Mary's worktable. Now that the important equipment in her lab was revived, and the ones beyond repair were thrown out, the lab looked rather empty. The briefcase we had found was on the table and we were staring at it, "What do you think that password could be?" Sahil asked, nudging Mary.

"How would I know?" She said.

Akito was tracing circles on the table with his finger. "How about we look into all the documents we have on him. Maybe it could be an equation that no one could solve. Or something personal only he knew about. Maybe there's a clue. I think we will leave that to you two. Sahil and I have stuff to do."

"We do?" Sahil asked and looked at Akito. And then at us. "Oh! Yeah! We do have to do that thing... with the... gotta go. Bye." He said and dragged Akito away with his hand.

Mary lent me a spare table and both of us plunged into studying parts of his life. He made his first invention a year after graduating with a Physics and Math double major along with minoring in AI programming, psychology and even Law.

She must have been a genius to study in so many fields and not completely lose her mind.

I looked up various things but could find anything remotely familiar. The name of Dr. Vikram's sister who was also a Physicist was brought up more than once, and I tried to deactivate the lock of the briefcase with it, but nothing happened. Strangely his sister's name was Nitya, a name which appeared somewhat familiar to me.

Well that was a given, considering I was looking into his early life. I rolled my chair over to where Mary was working and whispered into her ear. "Found anything?"

"Wow!" My eyes twinkled with amusement as she almost jumped out of her seat. "You scared the crap out of me, you idiot."

I chuckled and wrapped my arms around her waist, resting my chin on her shoulder and peered into the screen she was so intently staring at.

"I can't help but feel a sort of connection to him." She said.

"A connection?"I slowly whispered in her ear as my chin was still resting on her shoulder.

"Yeah. I don't know why though. It may be a coincidence that her wife looked exactly like me." She uttered and showed me Vikram's wife's picture.

"Yeah, you are correct." I said looking closely at the picture, but can there be any mysterious reason for it or just a coincidence.

"I don't know.", replied Mary. "Even we have no pictures of Dr. Vikram. After his death, his followers destroyed all his pictures, for unknown reasons."

"Maybe Dr. Vikram knew that in future if anyone wants to find the Universe Bomb then it should not be easy for him and therefore he has hidden most of the information."

"Say Mary, can you do me a favor?" I withdrew my chin from her shoulder and went to sit near her."

"Depends on what it is," she said playfully.

"Can you tell me more about yourself, I want to know more about your family, your past."

She stared at me with love for a moment then started after giving a sweet smile, "I love my parents just like everyone. I was very much connected to them as I am their single child. But things weren't going good for them. By 2290, both of them lost their jobs to AI. There was no income and they were getting very depressed but then also they took complete care of mine and fulfilled all my necessities and wishes. Even as a child I could sense that things weren't going well for us, I was just 6 when my parents were sent into the Dreamscape program - just like others who were unemployed and poor - of 2328. Though the Dreamscape program was active from 2298, my parents were sent late in it because their intellect was higher than average but till 2328, even they were sent because employment opportunities further decreased. My mother's last words were, 'Be happy, my child and do something good for society'." Mary completed and got emotional

I held her hands and wiped away her tears. Then she continued," Commander took me on his mission after that, along with Jessie, Sahil, Akito and others. We are really grateful to him for that."

"But did he really do the right thing? I mean... You all are just teenagers and he dragged you into this... this warzone." I asked, after enclosing Mary in my arms.

"Yes. He definitely did the right thing. We would have died of starvation or become petty thieves if he hadn't found us. He taught us the one thing we needed most in these times of turmoil, the art of self-defense. He paid for our education, made us strong, smart, empathetic. We are fighting to save the world and nothing can be better than it." She looked me straight in my eyes. After a moment of silence she said, "Besides, a life without parental love, it makes you stronger. I know it's cruel to let a child live without it, but without it a child matured faster and that is something we need today. But," she said holding my hands and with a smile. "It wasn't

as lonely as it may seem. I had friends. Sahil, Akito, Jessie and now you."
Her eyes twinkled when said 'you'. And I couldn't help but embrace her.
We cuddle for about 10 minutes.

"I wonder... what if we got married, and... had kids. I would give up my
job here and go live at one of the civilian camps with you," Mary said.

"We can build a house." I added.

"Oh. You know what? We will even have a pool. And, we will have a
garden on the terrace and we will spend all the evenings there." She said,
excited

I moved over and kissed her. "I love you Mary. I want to spend the rest of
my life with you."

She blushed. "So do I."

<div align="center">~~~~~~</div>

After a few hours (in time-machine):-

"Ah Leo. It's good to see you here," I turned to Sahil rushing to match my
pace. "I have to tell you something." Sahil seemed extremely strange. His
eyes were somewhat red, his tone and conduct were abnormal and
unnatural.

"What is it?"

"Well.... I know this must be hard for you to hear but... Mary doesn't love
you."

"What? What do you mean? Of course she loves me! She told me so
herself."
Sahil shook his head. "No. It's all a lie and deceit. I care about you Leo, so
hear me out. Mary is only pretending to love you so that you resolve

yourself to fight for our cause. She really loves Akito. Trust me I have known them my whole life."

"I don't believe you," I said pushing him away. It is the first time I got anguished with Sahil. I trust Mary and her love, I have no doubts, uncertainty or objections over that.

After just a few minutes, when I was heading toward Mary's lab, to clarify these questions of mistrust, I saw her entering Akito's room. Sahil's words started echoing in my mind. I walked toward the room and heard a lock being activated. I pressed my ear against the door from outside to hear what they were talking about.

"How could you propose to marry Leo? What is this Mary? I thought we love each other? Do you love Leo now?" Akito questioned.

Then, I heard Mary's voice.

"Hush! No way. As if I would ever love a guy I met barely two weeks ago. I love you. I've known you my whole life." I felt an ache spread in my heart. My throat started aching from holding back tears, but I felt my cheeks turn wet nonetheless. "I only played along with him because I didn't want to lower his strength and morale. If I tell him that I love you then he may get depressed and more after he wouldn't be able to fight for us at his fullest in war. Therefore, I thought to play with his feelings for some time so that we get an advantage in war and come out triumphant in it."

I clenched the fabric over my heart and dashed toward my room. Trying to distract myself, I tried to dig in deeper in Dr. Vikram's life. But my attempt was futile. I tossed the device on the table and dug my face into my pillow.

"Ammf." I screamed into my pillow and my tears soaked the it. I couldn't believe I never saw recognised their false love play. How could I let myself be played like that? How could that sweet and innocent-looking girl... How could Mary do this to me? I loved her truly from my heart.

Three hours later I heard a knock and Mary came inside. A smile was plastered on her face. If I didn't know any better, it would almost seem genuine.

She moved to wrap her arms around me but I swatted them away as if she was an annoying fly. The smile on her face fell and she looked at me with a confused expression. "Leo?"

"Get out of here. I don't want to see your face right now."

"What? Why?"

"I know! I know that you like Akito and that you have been leading me one just so that I will fight with full strength on your side. Well guess what, I would have done that even if you hadn't put me on this damned show. I would have been just fine. So get out of my sight!"

"I... I don't understand. What do you mean..." I threw her hand to her and started moving outside. I saw her face, extremely melancholic, as I moved out.

"I heard your conversation with Akito earlier. And don't want to talk to you anymore," I yelled and banged the door shut.

"Damn it." I punched the door with the side of fist and tears streamed down my eyes. Why did she do this to me?

~~~~~

I was walking toward Mary's lab with Sahil, when I saw Akito passing by. I broke away from Sahil and approached him.
~~~~~

"How could you do this to me?" I yelled.

"What?" He asked with his oh-so-perfect face. He didn't even look phased by it.

"I thought you were my friend. You loved Mary and you haven't told this truth to me. Truth not told is equal to a lie. If you would have told me then I might accept your relationship with Mary with grace. I am happy for you as you both make a good couple but you shouldn't have played with my feelings" I yelled, tears bursted in my eyes out of grief and anger.

"What? You think I and Mary.....?"

"Don't talk to me, you have broken my trust and faith in our friendship."

"Hey," I turned to see Sahil place a hand on my shoulder. "We should get going. You are causing a scene." I moved away. Today had to be the worst day of my life, at least of the life I remembered.

Almost four days passed with me completely ghosting Mariana and Akito. I was really upset with Mary as I had accepted that Mary would be Akito's but when she proposed to me and got connected to me, I felt my life around her and suddenly now I am feeling that my life is taken away from me. I'm feeling just like a dead man. I have cried a lot these days, even Mary has cried, I don't know why. Maybe she is trying to show me her concern but I am still not ready to forgive her. I didn't talk to them and whenever we were working together at the lab, I drowned out all sound by wearing noise canceling headphones Sahil had given me.

In the afternoon, a hologram of an extremely beautiful girl appeared in my chamber. The girl, even more beautiful and cute than Mary, said, "I'm a member of Thinker's group. I heard about how your feelings are hurt. I have always admired you as I have heard about what you did for Mary, taking her punishments, saving her life but what she gave you in return is extremely erroneous and malicious. I have liked you always and I'm here to show my feelings to you and give you an offer to join our group, if possible. So what do you think?"

I started pondering over it. She was extremely beautiful and from her words, she appeared caring, empathetic and one who really thinks about me.

Questions started clouding my mind, "So, can she be the right choice for me? Should I really leave Urja and join ReS?" She was still looking at me through her hologram . "I'm Lucy", she said.

After thinking for a few minutes I replied, "I'm grateful to you, Lucy, for your concern and happy to see that you care for me. You seem like a really caring, smart and attractive girl but my reply to your question is.....", I took a deep breath and continued, "I'm sorry, I can't love you. I have so deeply and emotionally connected to Mary that now I can be either hers or of no one's. I really hope that you get a partner better than me who will reciprocate your qualities and will love you a lot. Though, I know Mary hurt my feelings but my love for her is never-ending, and even if she deserts me, leaves me or kills me, I will love her forever, as I'm a true lover."

Lucy said, "It's really so romantic to hear that, I hope you get Mary's love and wish for your team's success." Her hologram disappeared.

In Thinker's Spaceship:

Lucy, "Your plan to fool Leo failed, he is still in love with Mary."

Thinker, "My plan is going perfectly. All pieces are set exactly as I want. Now, you all just see how we win this war." He laughs.

Mariana was devastated with the new development in Leo and her relationship. She didn't know what to do about Leo's misunderstanding.

There's no way she loved Akito. He was like a brother to her, and Leo didn't even give her a chance to explain.

Mary determined herself to fix things and started walking toward Leo's room to settle things with him. But was caught in her tracks when she saw Sahil heading toward the human teleporters with Dr. Vikram's briefcase in his hand.

She slowly sneaked into the room and soon as he disappeared from the platform, she jumped towards it before the coordinates reset.

After a flash of light and those of pain in her forehead, she found herself in a control room. It was filled with large screens and holographic devices. She crouched down and peeked from behind one of the tables.

"Your delivery, sir." Mary gasped as she saw Sahil walk toward a man with the briefcase in his hand. A woman stood beside him, with a devilish smile. She recognized her as The Thinker's wife. That meant he was...

"Sahil!" She yelled as she grabbed his wrist. "You can't give that to him!" She said as she pulled him to run with her. It soon became clear that he was hypnotized.

"Sahil! It's me, Mary." His eyes were still as distant as ever. How could she bring him back to reality? Then she remembered how last year he had been pestering her to call him big brother. It had seemed embarrassing to Mary so she had adamantly refused. But... desperate times called for desperate measures. "Big brother, please come back."

Sahil slowly comes back to reality after hearing the above words, 'Big Brother' from Mary.
"Wait. Where are we?" He asked. I will explain later. We have leave now?"

"Oh Shit!" He said. He probably remembered what he had done and he was immensely regretting it.

Mart turned to look at him, but saw that The Thinker's wife had aimed a gun at him. She pulled his arm toward her and moved behind him and was subjected to an electric shock. She screamed in agony as electricity filled her body. Dropping to the floor she started twitching uncontrollably. Her eyes met Sahil's and he knew what she meant immediately.

Mary said, "Go Sahil. We don't have time." She breathed heavily. "Tell Commander and our friends that I will always love them. Tell Leo that I loved him and will love him forever. Please make him happy and let us win the war." He couldn't just leave her in enemy territory. Who knew what those psychopaths would do to her. But he knew that there was no time. Thinker's subordinates were heading to the room as he hesitated to move. "I will make sure you won't die in vain." A small smile spread across her face as she breathed for the last.

"You will pay for what you have," Sahil yelled, with his eyes filled with tears, at The Thinker and teleported back in the time machine.

He rushed out of the teleporter room and moved to gather everyone.

As he stood on the commander's makeshift stage and explained to everyone what had happened. He felt Leo's gaze piercing him. He looked in his direction to see that his eyes were filled with tears and he seemed rather aggravated. After explaining the details of his encounter with the Thinker, he walked to Leo.

"Tell me, Sahil. About Mary and Akito..." I asked.

"What you see was an integration of AI programming and holograms. They weren't Mary and Akito, just their holograms along with their voice. I did it while I was hypnotized." He said, confirming my worst fears. I had been mad at Mary and didn't even talk to her for days. And now... now I could never talk to her. She was gone. Forever. And it was all Sahil's... no. I couldn't blame my best friend for that. I couldn't help but look at him with discontent. And I knew that he too blamed himself for it.

But... I didn't have the heart to console him. Because a part of me blamed myself, for not believing in Mary's love for me. I was a fool and although I couldn't correct my mistakes, I could at the very least, avenge her death.

I looked at the Commander walking to the stage. And I felt a huge jolt as the whole time machine shook. I stretched out my arms to balance myself, but fell down nonetheless. Sahil too lost his balance.

"My dear comrades," the commander started. "We are finally back in our time. Ready your weapons. All your gear. I believe their forces might be right outside our base. Resolve yourselves to fight. For the future of your children. For the future of your loved ones." The commander almost choked on his own words as he said, "for Mary."

I choked out a sob. I didn't even get the time to mourn for the death of the love of my life, but now I had to fight. Fight so that her sacrifice wouldn't be in vain. Fight so that she could rest in peace. I wiped off a tear rolling down my cheek and moved to grab a weapon for myself.

~~~~~~

After a few hours of turbulence, I and Sahil are sitting in the main chamber of the time machine along with the commander and other companions. We were making strategies for our battleships, our army and how can we approach the thinker's army, but suddenly someone came rushing in our room and said, "Thinker is going live and he is said to give a speech in front of all people, of all countries and even of space."

Commander said," IOT T.V. pls turn on and let us see Thinker's speech."

Suddenly in the air, a rectangular shaped framework of metal appeared and it started showing Thinker's speech. Thinker is present like a bright hero in a complete IOT suit and starts his speech.....
~~~~~~

Thinker started, "Good evening to all my dear intelligent creatures present on earth and in space. I am very grateful for the admiration of my fellow beings. It induces a very noble and proud feeling in my heart and I have always regarded my intellect as a gift given to me to serve my society, to upgrade our living standards, and to make this world a better place to live in. I consider that I have profoundly tried to establish my objectives and as a society we have developed from the past 40 years. I wholeheartedly thank the Presidents of all countries, and all the business tycoons of our universe who made me world leader and supported me to be the global coordinator. After the dreamscape mission, when I got the above mentioned position, I have always thought for the betterment of our world and have done all the work accordingly.

But from the past 5 years as everyone know there is some conflict between my team and another political party named "Urja", the later claims that The Great Thinker, that is myself, is not worthy to be the global leader and I am a big threat to the world, but my dear and lovely companions, you all have trusted me throughout my journey, at all phases of my career and today your faith in me has been proved true, as I and my team have got crystal clear evidences that Urja group has found the long-lost, mysterious and extremely catastrophic Universe bomb. Now their ulterior motives are coming to surface as the Urja group is planning to destroy our whole universe by the explosion of that bomb and making the "anti-matter wave crash" in our universe. They even killed my men who tried to persuade them to stop.

This will destroy everything but them, and when they will be saved, they will be the creators of the new universe which they want to rule. They will make a world, where they are Gods. This is completely immoral and inhumane but the thinker is still there to protect the world from such alien beings, from such malicious dreams. The world has to not fear from them, my army will do everything to defuse bomb and saving Humanity, but it's my my sincere request to everyone - to all the weapon developers, technology designers, business tycoons, coordinator and ultimately to all the people - do not support Urja group in any circumstance, do not believe in them, do not trust them over anything, as the world do not need them and we will not let them to be the Gods. Thanks".

We were all shocked after hearing it. Wrong claims have been made over us I was already anguished but after this which I got ferocious out of patience and my only thought was how can a person be so devil but from inside and so godly from outside it's not us who want to destroy Universe, it's not us who want to be Gods, it's him only and only Thinker, The Thinker, but how can we prove this to our world as all the intelligent minds remaining in the world have great loads of faith in him. Commander also looked distressed and everyone in the room seemed to be in panic, not even us but every one of our group were frightened.

Commander went to talk to all the weapon suppliers and finance providers over this matter. Then he came and said many weapon suppliers have broken their partnerships with us. We even lack funds and by that time he came we received approximately 2000 applications from members of our group who wanted to exit it. Our group suddenly got in a fragile condition and we were not able to think: 'what to do next'. Commander said, "Akito is with other members on Earth of 2340 and he is trying to manage situations over there. We should go to our base camp and think of the future strategies there."

Our time-machine finally came into the future:- Year 2340. It is the present for my companions as they belong from this timeline. Our base was formed on 1 of Saturn's moon, it was the most fertile, most resourceful and most architecturally perfect moon of our Solar System, making it the most ideal location for our camp. Our base was extremely giant, just like a scene from a sci-fi movie, but it's not a movie, it's reality. Our team has around half-a-million people but fear is noticeable on everyone's face, as Thinker's speech has destroyed our previous strategies and plans.
Commander finally began to encourage everyone and remind us of our situation, " The time has finally come. This is the time for which I prepared for you from the past 20 years. This is the time where we are directly standing in front of our enemy and just a few inches away from

accomplishing our dreams. We dreamt of making Earth: Humanitarian, Place of Love and affection, and we can finally do so by defeating Thinker's army, and by deactivating Universe Bomb and thereby saving Humanity. I know we lack in funds, in resources, in weapons and even in numbers of members. But we surpass Thinker and his men in strength, in hope, in spirit, in ambition, in purity of our dreams. I know many of you may be scared as this war may take lives of prestigious souls but remember this sacrifice will be eternal and will be remembered by everyone with the slogan of, "The Heavenly Creatures who save Humanity." I have never and will never force anyone to accept this invitation of joining war from Urja group, not just war, a revolutionary movement to save Humanity, but I will surely promise all of you that your contributions in war will never be forgotten and your sacrifice will never get wasted....... Thinker's army is coming to seize Bomb briefcase from us but we won't let it happen. We will find the voice password and then deactivate it but till then we have to fight against them. We will not fight for people who don't trust us, but we will fight for ourselves, our family and friends, and for Humanity. So, who is with me?"

I thought, "Mary always wanted us to be happy but before that she always expected us to do everything required to help others, to make others' happy. Today, I will fulfill her wish. I will fight for Mary." Tears ran through my eyes.

I shouted, "I'm with you." Everyone accompanied me by shouting, "We are with you.".
Again, "We are... With you." No one left the group after this speech.

Commander assigned everyone their task and as I have studied a myriad of stuff about Dr. Vikram, I went in the Bomb defusing team and we started finding Briefcase's voice password.
After half-an-hour our sensors started receiving signals of someone approaching us from Jupiter. It can be easily guessed that it's Thinker's army. They were approaching us in their advanced spaceships at very high speed. It looked like this:-

But we made an amazing strategy to help us. So, as spaceships come near us in the range of 100 km, we focused artificial lights of very high intensity on those spaceships which will make the pilot blind for some time. As the pilot got blind, it struck our space-mine (similar to land-mine) and then a huge explosion took place. This way many spaceships of the opposite group got destroyed. The light from the explosion looked like this:-

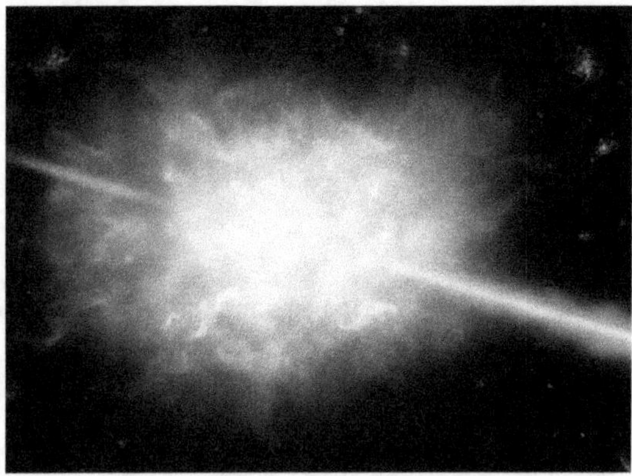

I asked Sahil, "How many human pilots would have died due to these blasts?" I felt pity on them but this is a part of War.

Sahil said, "None. Spaceships are auto driven. As I told you about A.I., these spaceships also run on A.I."

Then we covered our moon and base with the help of a shield (Transparent Energy shield). But resources required to completely enclose the complete moon weren't available and therefore the back side of the moon wasn't covered. It will allow the entrance of enemies once they detect this loophole. So, the Commander decided to go from here to Earth in 2340, and defuse the bomb there. But when we started evacuation, Thinker's spaceships had almost detected the loophole and started going to that side to come inside.

Commander said, " Everyone of you make it fast. Till then I will stop the spaceships."

But Frian (one of our team members) argued, "Sir you can't die. Team needs you. I and my team will stop them, you all evacuate from here."

The Commander's eyes got filled with tears and we continued shifting from the spaceships.

When I, Commander and a few other members got settled in the last spaceship to go to Earth, Frian, Rose, Sophie and their team members also got ready in spaceships to fight the A.I. shuttles and stop them. One A.I. shuttle was just about to fire its beam on us but just at that point Sophie came in between along with his fighter spaceship to save us, and her spaceship got blasted."

We came to Earth at the speed of Sound and landed in the Sahara Desert where Team Urja has made infrastructure for its base on Earth. It wasn't looking like a Desert anymore but just equivalent to New York - having skyscrapers and facilities - as Sahil in our journey told me that Team Urja's many members are employed here.

It was the first time I had actually stepped into the lands of the twenty fourth century. It was an absolute disaster. Our base buildings had either been blown off with explosives or crumbled in on itself with erosion.

"All the civilians have been evacuated," Akito said.
I stared at him and said, "Akito. I am sorry about-"

"Don't worry. I completely understand. You were going through a lot back then."
I saw that his eyes had lost their shine. And it was the first time I had ever seen him so disheveled. His hair was a mess, there were bags under his eyes. "Sahil, Jessie, Mary and I, we grew up together under the Commander's watch. We are like siblings to each other." He said. "I really miss Mary, but we will take her Revenge."

"Yes. We will " I spell enthusiastically along with melancholy. With that, he left for the front lines. Sahil came beside me.

After a long pause, he said, "let's go."

I grabbed what looked like an M24 but was actually a gun that shot electricity over large distances. I wore rubber gloves to prevent being subjected to the shocks myself and some other small weapons were stuffed into my flannel bag. But when I looked up and almost dropped my gun. My eyes widened and a gasp escaped my mouth. Saturn's moon, our base... it exploded. That means Frian, Rose and all others have died… Tears were there in the eyes of everyone along with a spirit to take revenge.

I looked at Sahil and he said that I have Mary's weapon. The one that Mary had made and because of which she was about to get punishment, it is now modified and used in actual war by me. In the complete war, just Mary's face was shining in my thoughts and tears in my eyes. I told her that I will be with her everyday but I doubted her and now she is not there..... I think she really made a wrong choice in making me her lover.... - Tears kept running through my eyes - I should not have doubted her, I should have always trusted her.

Now in our base camp, the war has already started and in some places, we were fighting with Thinker's army, who included A.I. Robots and a few people who lead those Robots regiments. Our army too has robots but not of the same power, strength and even less in number....... extremely less.

So Commander and Akito made a plan in which our Robots will be divided in various groups and each group will contain some robots along with people and will be called a regiment. We were thus divided in various small regiments, all-round Sahara Desert and everyone took a weapon from various alternatives. I was with Akito. I wore an IOT war suit, just like the one I saw in Avengers - Iron Man, but I never thought that Iron Man Suit would be worn by me for a war. After wearing a helmet, it included inbuilt communication and other technological devices.

"Yes. I will be heading there right away," I heard Sahil say through his brain fit communication device.

"Follow me." Akito said
We started running on a fly over. The flyover had broken down and the way up was a steep slope of broken concrete. I didn't know how safe it was but I climbed nonetheless. When we were on the top, I looked down to see dust blinding my vision. They were here. People, on vehicles the likes of which I had never seen before, they were rushing toward us. I saw other members of URJA line up at the fly-over and started to set up sniping guns.

"We are members of the sniping team. We are to assist the ones who are on the front lines," Sahil said. "We are also the last line of defense. If worse comes to worst, we defend our base and this baby, The Briefcase" He said patting Dr. Vikram's briefcase. He continued, "Some members are still working in a few places to find the voice password and once they find it, the war will be over as we will defuse it but till then its mine team's duty to keep it safe.

I set up my gun and looked through the scope and watched Akito use laser guns from which the emitted laser is killing 10 to 20 robots at an instance. I saw no hesitation in his movements. A shudder went down my spine. "Had he killed before?", I asked Sahil

"In today's world. It's inevitable. You must kill to survive," Sahil said and finally went with his team and briefcase.

Now I, Akito and our regiment along with other regiments reached their accurate position. Regiments of Robots along with few people, high speed automatic air-crafts, and disastrous weapons can be seen from here.

Finally the Commander said, "Let them know the lightning of the Urja group. Attack everyone."

We all started running with our weapons. I saw Jessie - using a teleporter and suddenly jumping behind the robot and finally melting it using her heat blast gun. I saw Grammy (another teammate) using U.V. guns, finally leading to a blast of Robots. I used my M24 and shot electricity, and destroyed some robots.
The gun also had a scope facility by which we can fire electricity even at long distances. I saw in the gun's scope that Akito was struggling with an opponent who was leading Robots. Opponent is using a dangerous "Splinter" (a beam which reacts with our body and breaks it to small fragments). I took aim and shot my electricity beam at the opponent and finally killed him. I shouted, "It's for Mary..... Revenge."

I moved the scope to another side of the battle and saw Jessie using a rifle to shoot what looked like acid at people. I soon realized that it was the toxic slime she had been working on the last time I went to her lab. This slime disrupts the A.I. programs of Robot, causing its ultimate failure. She seemed like she needed no help.

Moving the scope further to the right I saw someone I didn't know struggling with enemy ammunition. It was obvious that he was on our side as all of us had tied a green piece of cloth on our arms. I shot at the people hounding him and a ball of electricity escaped the nozzle of my gun and twitching, the men fell to the ground. I saw the guy from our team shoot a salute in our general direction and continued to fight.

As time passed the grounds filled with dead bodies and kept watching. The scent of blood was reaching all the way from down there.

Suddenly some robots identified that Akito is one of the Team's main fighters and therefore they started focusing on him. When they got the chance, they fired an itch - a microbe missile - at him and he started itching seriously. Sahil finally shot Akito as the death with an itch was worse than a normal death.

"No! No" I looked at Sahil's horror stricken face and melancholic eyes through my gun's scope. I started fumbling with my gun to find what he was looking for and when I finally spotted it, my hands ran cold with terror. Lying on the ground, with blood soaking his abdomen was Akito. His hair was stuck to his face with sweat and blood and he seemed to be vomiting blood as well. I rotated my scope to zoom in and saw the light leave his eyes. He is saying to Sahil, " Take care of Commander, Leo and others. And let us win." His breath stopped. He was gone. I fell on butt as the horror took over me. The guy I had grown so close to as time passed by. The guy I was jealous of but also admired. Akito... was gone. Tears rose back in my eyes. Seriously, how can I be such a fool who can easily become a puppet of a Thinker. I'm very sorry Akito for all my wrong deeds.

Our various regiments were fighting courageously and we hoped that this time we could win the battle. But suddenly something unexpected happened.

"Leo," Sahil said through the inbuilt device of the suit, choking on his own voice. "We don't have time to mourn." He mah have noticed me mourning

"But Akito..." i uttered

"I know. I am sad as well. But... if we stay like this, more people would meet their end... giving them more time to search for the voice password of the briefcase is the least we can do."

Sahil wasn't carrying a briefcase as he said that he had given it to one of his regiment members. We again got back to our regiments and took our positions.

Suddenly, the earth beneath us started shaking. Everyone stopped and got confused over what was happening. It shook very hard and sand quivered, many robots of our team submerged in shaking sand(as the artificially constructed road on Sahara got vandalised). Finally in front of my regiment, a small nano-aircraft (just like a smaller version of a remote-controlled plane) appeared. Everyone except me was petrified saying, "It's a nano-bomb..... Run away." This way everyone started running here and there to be alive. One nano-bomb got stuck to a member in front of me and then it blasted with that member and other 3 to 4 near him, I got a big thrust from the explosion and landed after 5 to 10 meters. I really got hurt from it and I wasn't able to move my left hand.

These nano-bombs continued to come from the interior of earth until all our regiments got disorganised.
After those nano-bombs, drilling robots appeared from the interior. They started firing heat on our team, most of our robots were destroyed, our people were killed and displaced because of it. Then a few people from the opposing team come surrounded by heavily-armed robots, who have

control of something. I tried to shoot them with my electric gun but couldn't aim properly as my left-hand wasn't giving support. Sahil came to help me as he sensed my pain. Really some emotional connections with friends can be so deep that they sense your pain even before it hurts you. It aroused tears in my eyes, and love in my heart for Sahil. If Mary had been there, I would have told her that friends like hers are extremely rare in this modern time.

Sahil said, "Come on Leo, you are fighting very well. Keep doing it."

I saw him, his left eye was damaged, his right hand was almost paralised. He could barely move properly but he is not ready to give up. I got charged up seeing his condition and pain.

" Are we winning this battle?" I asked.
He gave me a cheeky grin. "We are going through a critical stage. Our regiments are misplaced. It's really astonishing that Thinker never goes to war but he is very good at making strategies as it really made our team very weak. If he had used his intellect in good work, he would have been proven a very good resource for the world. "

I asked, "So what we will do if we lose?"
I thought, "What would I say to Mary about the war in heaven? She sacrificed herself for World. We have to win anyhow."

Suddenly there was a thunderous sound of explosion approximately 20 miles away. At the sound of a huge explosion I looked at its source. "Holy-" The entire left flank had been wiped out. "What... what is that."

"Quantum bombs. Ten times stronger than nuclear bombs," he explained. I shuddered.

Night had already fallen and visibility was close to nil but our suit adjusted with the Night vision glasses.

My eyes were fixed on the battlefield when it happened. I heard many gasps and screams of terror and when I turned to see that all of them were looking at the sky.

In the commotion the enemy forces managed to turn the tide in their favour and started marching upon us. "Back to the base team. Equip yourself with close combat weapons." Jessie's voice came from the communication device they had given me. I ran through the stand and slid down the broken flyover and toward the base. I asked Jessie, "What does she mean by that statement?"

She said, "Our weapons are out of power, therefore we have to choose some weapons which are left with power or which consume less power."

I pulled out the weapon that I had been learning to use in my free time. Mary taught me how to use this sword, I will use it to kill those, ones who killed Mary. I took my lazer sword and cut the legs of an opponent as he marched into our base, he fell to the ground and a fellow URJA member shot him through his heart. Robots were not used at night as A.I. fails in night vision.

I swung my sword another time and this time, it's sharp end dug into the man's throat and slit it. Blood sprang out of it and the man, wide eyed fell to the floor. Before I could even feel the shock of ending a life I took another and another and another. Tears filled my eyes at what I had become. A murderer. And in this train of thought, I lost my composure and my defenses fell.

I saw someone shooting an electric shot at me. I put my hands in front of my face and braced myself for impact, but instead, I heard a male yelp of pain.

I opened my eyes to see... "Commander!" I dashed toward his falling body. "Why... why did you jump in front of me?"

The man smiled. "What is the life of a dying old man worth? Your life is much more important."

"You are the commander. How could my life be more important than yours?" I asked as tears filled my eyes.

"Look around yourself, what do you see?" I did, everyone was fighting. There was death everywhere. I looked at the commander. A blow to the stomach. It was something that would kill him slowly. A painful death.

"Look at the man who tried to kill you." I did. He was already dead.

"He was killed by one of his own."

I looked and indeed saw none of our soldiers there. "Why?"

"Leo..." the commander gasped in pain. "It seems that The Thinker has issued a no kill order for you."
"Why?"

"It seems he has some different plans for you." I looked at him, confused. "You see, Leo. You are a major effect on the timeline. Your death would change the timeline."

"I... I don't understand, commander."

"Just remember, Urja wanted peace not war. I trust you my son from the 1st day, you have done enough research on Dr. Vikram, you can find the voice password and save the world...... You are Leo - The Saviour......The...." before he could finish, he choked on his breath, and... passed away. I blinked off my tears and shut his eyes with my hand.

I turned around and saw that Sahil too was on the floor bleeding. I rushed to him. "Sahil!"

"Leo," he gave me a pained smile. Blood was dripping down his forehead. His outgrown hair was stuck to his cheek with dried blood. And blood was rushing out of his shoulder. "I was a hero, wasn't I?" Sahil said to see my laugh at his end.

I nodded my head furiously as tears streamed down my eyes.

"Do... do you think Mary will forgive me. I... I left her in the enemy base. She died because of... me." Sahil said in between gasps of pain.

"I am sure when she said that she loved us, she meant you too. You fought courageously Sahil, you have done a great job, now just relax". I said so as his heart beat was decreasing and my IOT-integrated A.I.-night vision helmet showed that he was about to die.

He smiled. "Really?"

"The briefcase... it's on that counter," he said pointing to his right.
"Don't say anything. Be at peace, Sahil," I said in between sobs.

He grabbed my hand. "Don't let all these deaths be in vain. You have to take care of your Briefcase and save the world....."

He clutched his shoulder and tears filled his eyes. "Leo... Leo, Don't cry, my life's purpose was to make people happy with my humour. At my death also, I want you to be happy. Smile please." He said with great concern. But... but I couldn't do anything, tears were automatically flowing down my eyes. I finally smiled for him.

He said, "Yeah.... That's my boyyy...." He never completely spelt his last word. With a loud gasp, his life too, ended. All noises around me drowned out. Fear and loneliness danced with what was left of my heartstrings. A flood of emotions came over me and I had no idea how to deal with them. Everyone I knew and loved in this timeline was dead. Will I ever be able to recover? What should I do now?

I bit my lip to fight back my tears but nothing helped. The grief far overshadowed any physical pain. I ran towards the briefcase and held it tight.

I felt a hand on my shoulder and I turned to see a man. Someone I had never seen before. I looked around me. The only people left were the ones that obediently stood behind him.

A smile cracked his face. "Who are you?" I asked.

"I believe in the ranks of URJA, they call me the Thinker."

I jumped up and ran towards him in anger. I was stopped by his men just three steps away from him. "You... you killed Mary. I will kill you"

"Who is that?"

The bastard didn't even know her name.

"You must be who they call Leo, correct?" He chuckled at my angry expression. "Come on. We have a lot to discuss."

"He sat down on a advanced tech IOT chair and his men pushed me to sit on another."

"You know how the villains love their victory speeches. I know you see me as one. But I'm not a villain. I just want to reconstruct the Universe in a much better way with my wife and my men." he said.

"Why do you need that bomb?" I asked angrily

"To destroy everything and create a better world."

"One that dances on your strings?" I asked, anger clear as glass on my face. He laughed out loud. "Tell me... if that bomb explodes everything, how do you plan to survive?" I asked

Thinker explained, "I am sure you have heard of the energy shield within the Briefcase. Well, the mechanism created to destroy the energy barrier in the Universe, to allow anti-matter wave influx, the energy shield of the briefcase is also made from the same substances. Whoever detonates the bomb and those in physical contact with him are covered with the same material the barrier is made of. And they are protected from the darn explosion."

"Dr. Vikram wouldn't have wanted that." I responded

"You are right. After all, he was a huge optimist. He wanted to save the world and be the hero. That guy who loved humanity more than probably even his family." He said

I asked, "But how will you create the Universe again?"

Thinker said, "That's not your matter of concern. I know exactly how to do so and I want to keep that with me. But I will explain to you how your destiny was controlled exactly by me."

"You see... everything that has happened in your life in the twenty fourth century is by the calculations of your truly. I will explain everything to you in detail. Firstly, you got in Urja's time-machine, do you think it was an accident? No..... Haha.." he laughs, "This was the starting of my great plan, to bring a teenager to the team of Urja, then you developed love for a girl, and by taking the punishment of her mistake, you two got further close. Her weapon was manipulated by one of my men as a part of a plan. I made the love bond develop between you two. Then you became a part of the team and founded the Briefcase. I have calculated this earlier only and therefore I hypnotised Sahil to break the love bond between you and bring me the suitcase. I would have easily defeated Sahil, after the death of your loved one, but I let him go, because I knew that when he would go back, the Urja group would start preparing for War and would lack resources after which they would ultimately lose the war." He laughs too hard.

A woman came near his chair and said, "Yes my love.... We will finally win the war and accomplish our mission." She would be Thinker's wife, which I can guess by listening to this.

I really got shocked listening to his plans. But I made a plan to still win ultimately. I spotted Jessie behind Thinker's men. I clenched my fist and my suit's metal hand shot out ropes that gouged out the eyes of the men who were holding me down. In the commotion, I snatched the briefcase from Thinker. Jessie by that time took an electric gun and aimed it at her wife.

The Thinker laughed. "What will you even do with it? That thing is made of an indestructible polymer. You won't be able to destroy it with your bare hands. And you little Commander of Urja, what do you want to do with my wife?" He laughs

His wife said, "My love, I think this girl is mad, she can even shoot me."

I said, "Yes, she will shoot your wife unless you let us go."

The Thinker said, "Yeah, I'm listening." Suddenly from his IOT chair, a metal hand came and spontaneously took a heat gun from the ground and shot both Jessie and his wife. Both got burnt and finally died.

I shouted, "What..... You killed your own wife and Jessie." Tears were still flowing but my eyes have now become completely dry.

He got strangely melancholic and said, "I have calculated this possibility before only. I prepared myself for this sacrifice to achieve the greater good for the world. To make the world a better place to live in."

I am able to see a few drops of tears in his eyes. I shouted, "How can this be better for the world. You have no feelings for anyone. How will you make a better Universe with this attitude?"

Thinker said in a gloomy tone, "Feelings. This is the biggest drawback of Humans. Without feelings, we can achieve the impossible, we can be extremely advanced, and we can gain unimaginable success. World doesn't need feelings. Development is the goal of human life but our feelings don't let us achieve that goal to its fullest. After destroying this Universe, I will make a Universe where there will be no feelings, everyone will just work for the betterment of the World and thus we will make Earth as good as Heaven. This is my dream for which I've been working for the past 100 years."

I started thinking about his verdicts and said, "You may be somewhat right but our feelings don't make us weak, it makes us strong as feelings only help us to feel brotherhood, love, affection and after all Humanity. Even Dr. Vikram wanted the world to be made with Humanity and not Success."

When I spoke above lines, I got glances of the ideologies and philosophies of Dr. Vikram, which I studied and recalled that he once said that, "I want people to chase Humanity and not Success. I have devoted my life to this thought and I am pleased to devote all my researches, inventions, businesses, and achievements to the same thought."

I thought I got the voice password for a briefcase which can be Dr. Vikram's quote on humanity and his purpose of life. I pressed the voice password switch in my suitcase and yelled:-

"We are Human Beings only when we work to reduce sufferings not just of ours but of everyone in the world. By this we will feel ultimate Happiness and satisfaction in life!" I yelled.

The Thinker's face contorted with shock and fear. The suitcase produced a voice, "You got the right password", then it slowly opened. The in it, there was a green screen showing some coordinates, maybe of the barrier and then there was a switch of "Enter", and the instructions written there read that pressing Enter will start the barrier destruction, and within about 15 mins, complete Universe will blast in a ball of energy if the antimatter wave is not stopped. I was unable to think of anything, this was supposed to be our goal as the Commander said that once we open the briefcase, we will find a way to defuse it but there is no path visible to do so. "What should I do now", is the only question hitting my mind.

After a few minutes, Thinker again started laughing. His laughing is now making me frightened. He started saying, "What you thought was that you will defeat me with your negligible intellect. I already knew exactly this moment from the start. Reaching this moment was only the goal of my grand plan. I knew that after the death of your love-bird, you will become ferocious and you will use your complete intellect to calculate the password of your briefcase and after opening it, you will have no choice but to hand it over to me. Everything happened just the way it was planned." He laughs. "If my love would be here, he would have been so happy to see me achieving this success. Now we are going towards a new Universe."

I got blank. I was able to think of nothing. The Thinker said, "Now just handover the briefcase to me. It's useless for you. You can neither defuse it nor use it to destroy the Universe because if you destroy Universe, you will alone be left there for eternity and that would be worse than a hellish punishment."

I really had no idea of what to do. I closed my eyes. I got a glance of Mary. I asked her, "I'm sorry my love. I wasn't able to save you, neither Commander, nor the Universe. I failed."

Mary said (in my mind), "One is defeated when one accepts defeat. You can still win. Just think, the solution is in front of you. Just remember whatever happens from now, trust yourself. I will always be proud of you and will love you forever whether I'm with you or not."

Her words opened my mind. I with no second thought "Pressed the ENTER key of the briefcase which destroyed the barrier and let the anti-matter wave inside our Universe."

I was shielded by a green barrier as I was able to see it. Thinker shouted loud, extremely loud, just like what a person does before his death. He said, "What have you done? You know that now you will be left alone in the Universe. You will live like you're cursed."

I said, "That is fine but I can't let World have a God like you. I can't let people feel feeling-less as my love, my Mary, told me that Feelings are what make us stronger, if not smarter. World needs those who have a heart, not just a mind. I am ready to suffer from anything for my Mary and I'm not like you who will sacrifice my love for my dream, but I will sacrifice my dreams, my life for my love".

Thinker stood from his smart chair and sat on the floor, near his wife and said, "I never knew that the emotions of a teenage boy could get in the way of my master plan. I never knew that emotions are so strong and can make one ready to suffer for eternity. I think my grand plan which was perfect till now was erroneous as I haven't considered the value of emotions in my calculations." His face was expressionless just like his men and army. He said at last, "The barrier will keep you alive when everything ends. Just close your eyes as within two minutes, our solar system is going to explode in lightning and this can make you blind."

His advice for the first time sounded really genuine and so I followed it and closed my eyes. When I was closing my eyes, my last vision was that I saw Jupiter exploding and his men were slowly disappearing and small amounts of energy was getting formed here."

"I truly loved the world, you know." He said at last.

The universe... has been finally destroyed.

CHAPTER 8
THE GREEN ENERGY

It's all dark and gloomy. Leo survived after the explosion of the bomb, as Thinker was right. The one who presses the trigger button in the briefcase actually gets surrounded by a protective shield of energy as created by Dr. Vikram. Now Leo finds himself in space with no living creatures, no earth, just black space(as depicted in movies) with few triangular lights which can be inferred as stars far far away. No noises, no discussions, just utter silence. He is startled and confused to be the only existing human left in such a vast universe. He is trapped in a web of unanswered questions and jumbled mysteries he can't unravel. All the matter is destroyed and converted to energy but the energy is scattered in the Universe and the teenager is able to see it, the energy looks like rays, or clusters of stars.

Leo thinks, I found myself amidst the twinkling stars as every element of the universe is destroyed, trying to decode the reason behind my solitary existence in the universe. I was in deep confusion about my lone survivor. Tons of questions smacking my mind,

"Where are the others with whom I was a few moments ago?"
"Did they disappear?"

"Are they in a similar situation like me?"
"Has everyone else died?"
OR
"AM I DEAD?"

I was panicked and nerve wrecked as this thought hit my mind. A shiver of horror passed through my body. I was in a dilemma when I thought of being dead. A bunch of emotions emanated from my heart. There was nothing around me except the twinkling stars that I saw from the roof of my house and today I'm amongst them. They were actually brighter than they appeared.

"Hey, Is anybody there?" I shouted. My voice just went far but there was no reply. I was terrified of being alone in a dark Universe. I tried to make my mind busy before I think about what is happening.

Suddenly, there were various constellations or something like them far away that made me fascinated and one of them resembled a newspaper. I had an immediate flash of my father. Various old memories of my time (2021) started hitting me. I now remembered the first time he taught me how to ride my favorite bicycle and all those deep conversations with him, be it anything about life and his proficient response to it as if he knew all the theories of the world. There was always a layer of calmness over his face no matter whatever happens in his life. For me, my father is and will always be my idol. How could I ever forget the perfect couple my father and mother made.

Tears arose in my eyes as, "I missed my momma, as it's been almost half a year since I saw him. I remembered how she ran behind me to feed me all the delicacies she cooked. I thought of my happy times when I came from school and my mother patted me and caressed my hair while asking how my day had been. She always used to put a "kaala teeka" over my head to protect me from being jinxed. My mother was the greatest source of support that I could ever have. Oh, how they used to pamper me and fulfill all my wishes and praise me for my little efforts embraced with a tinge of hard work, how they helped me learn word by word and made me into what I am today. I'm getting really emotional as I have so many things to say to my mom but she is not with me. I have never been out of her sight for so long." Tears kept floating down my eyes but I calmed myself and said to myself, "You have to be strong. Remember what your mom has taught you. Never lose hope, it is the biggest strength."

I had a glimpse of all those cackles and giggles on the dining table when my complete family sat together for dinner. I pondered about those moments and believed that it was the golden period of my life. This nostalgia made my heart skip a beat and a couple of tears unrolled from my swollen eyes.

Meanwhile these thoughts tangled my mind, I suddenly could hear my mumma's voice. Oh! Her voice was as sweet as honey and the buckets of love she showered on me when she called out my name. She is saying, "My dear son. The apple of my eyes. I've always guided you to seek the path that is right for you. And right things are always criticized before they are valued. The path of righteousness always has hurdles that are very tough to cross. It may be in the form of emotions that chain you from moving forward. But whatever it is, you are my strong boy. Fight every obstacle with strength and courage." Those were her last words that striked the eardrum of my ears.

I could not control my feelings and was on the verge of bursting out into uncontrollable tears. My heartbeat almost sank. I miss her terribly.
The next star-like light I came across is like a round circular ball of fire. This obviously had to be my chubby sister Nitya and her love for snowball fights. I terribly missed her. She has been my partner in crime since the very beginning of our lives. Though we had always been quarreling and messing with each other, yet all the good moments spent with her jingled through my thoughts. I was petrified by the mere imagination that it was my last snowball fight with her.

For a moment, I thought about the peace I felt when I used to listen to music for many hours a day and went to the rooftop in the evening to gaze at the beautiful colors the sky displayed each day. It was so soothing and a reviving hour of the day for me. I talked to plants and flowers during my free time as I believed it helped them grow faster and better. I listened to the chirping birds and glared at the dancing trees during the sundown. At night I would stargaze and think about the times I had lived my life to the fullest. I enjoyed the cracking sound of heavy rains while sipping in my favorite black coffee and reading a novel. On the other days, I would just stand in the balcony and revive the boisterous beauty of Manali I had been seeing since childhood. Indeed living in the land of snow is one of the blessings God can ever bestow upon you. It took me away from all the hassles of life and made me explore a whole new different world. A wave of happiness surrounded my thoughts.

A group of stars were twinkling together on a different side of the space. It was as bright as a button. Seeing them, I got a flashback of how me and all my friends from time travel made a circle and discussed our ideas to find out about the universe bomb. Their mind blowing ideas would have emitted a light as bright as those stars I see. It is so fascinating and thrilling to recall how we made memories out of the times we had been searching for the most destructive structure- the universe bomb.

I thought about how we went to unexplored places we had never seen before and the amazed expressions my friend, Akito had each time. Everyone were awestruck when they went to new places and discovered something new about the universe every time. I smiled over how Sahil made us laugh on every little occasion by cracking jokes.

There was one brightest star I gazed upon when I was jumbling across all of them. It's sheer brightness and sparkling view just made one face appear in my mind.

The epitome of beauty my eyes had witnessed when I first met her. Her hazy brown swirls sticking to her face, her big bold grey eyes and the way she smiled! I bet it seemed as if thousands of sunflowers had blossomed in the bright cheer of sunshine. Her aura was absolutely enthusiastic and pleasing. Her velvety eyelashes and her fair complexion made her look no less than a Barbie doll.

And I precisely remember and blushed over the face my love marina made when she saw me and the other girls chit chatting in the corner. She became green with envy when she saw me talking to any other girl. Indeed I held a special place in her life.

But then I was filled with deep groan and grief as I felt anguished by the demise of my sweet Mary. I felt helpless as no energy could bring her back to life. I cursed the group one for their actions. These bittersweet moments made me emotional and nervous both at the same time as I was presently left alone in this universe.

It's rightly said that you start valuing something when you see it going away from you. My body shivered and trembled by the mere thought of losing the ones with whom I had been since these past years. A sheer stark terror seized me, terror that knows no understanding, terror that knows no control, terror that no one can understand until they experience it themselves. I recognized the value of emotions I have towards my closed ones when I was left in isolation. I was as quiet as a mouse when the flood of such thoughts hit me.

The silence is suddenly disrupted by a sharp noise that arises out of nowhere. I suffer from palpitations and I got confused about this unanticipated quivering. My face is convulsed with fear and his eyes, red and teary. I looked here and there to trace the origin of this weird happening.

I was astonished to witness a green ray of light sparkling from a far flung spot that captured my attention. It gradually became darker. I was in deep thoughts already and now had another set of questions, troubling me with the sight of that sparkle.

I started moving towards it to find out the origin of that bright green torch-like light appearing in front of my eyes. As I neared to it, I asked it,

"Who are you?"

"What is your name?"

"What are you doing here?"

Before I could ask any further, a deep muffled voice started echoing all over the place. It said, "Hello teenager."

I got baffled and said, "You are an energy then also you can speak. How's that possible?"

Energy said, , "Yes, I can speak.

I'm the one who exists,
In this universe for a long time.
All the life forms you see today,
I'm the reason behind them-bold and prime.
Me and my mate light,
Mixed together to form everything.
From these Galaxies, stars, moon and sun,
To those planets and their rings."

I felt as if he had heard this kind of statement somewhere. With a quick flash, the thought of the big bang theory strikes his mind. He asks the green light, " Are you talking about the famous big bang theory??"

The green rays replied, "Yes, my dear teenager. You guessed it right. I'm that tiny point which gave existence to this vast life form. I'm an intangible form of energy that brings out the best in someone and gives rise to gazillions of emotions. I bring along with me bundles of feelings like happiness, hope, joy, peace, contentment, excitement, encouragement and satisfaction. I'm that element of life which gives someone a new attitude towards achieving his goals, following his dreams and living his life to the fullest. I'm present in every creature of this universe and my existence is inseparable, either I'm visibly felt or I need to be found."

"I'm a POSITIVE ENERGY!"

I, in utter confusion, asked, "Sorry but I'm not able to understand anything. Can you explain once again."

Green energy started explaining, "Before this material universe, before the objects in space, the universe just consisted of energies. These energies are not the one which humans study(not like kinetic, solar, etc). These were actually positive emotional energies which existed in the universe and occupied the complete volume of the universe; these energies, including me, interact by exchanging emotions with each other, not the emotions which humans like you feel, but you can understand these emotions as a form of communication.

This is how we look:

This way the harmony of the universe was maintained. This process kept going for billions of years in which various positive energies existed and expanded. We created new types of energies from our mutual exchange of emotions and kept the universe expanding but suddenly something undesired happened. Among these positive energies started developing a few energies which had extremely negative emotions. These negative emotions energy started decaying and collapsing with positive energies leading to imbalance in the universe and disrupting the harmony of energies. As I said, all the energies had a conscious mind just like what humans have and so all the positive energies communicated with each other using synapses of emotions to answer how to solve this problem of negative energies and finally we all came to a conclusion that we must change our form to matter. In this way the positive energy will exist but in a different form and will be spread all around the Universe so we did the same and that is what is known as the Big Bang theory in which positive energies exploded and changed to matter and kept the harmony of the Universe flowing."

I was fascinated to know such things, "It's amazing. I never knew it."
I asked, "So, Thinker and his group knew of your existence as they believed after the destruction of the bomb, they would be able to create a new Universe?"

Green energy, "No, that's not right. No one knows my existence as we are not yet discovered. What would happen after the end of the Universe, no one knew exactly. It was just a mystery and everyone had various assumptions about it. Thinker would have calculated that the blast will result in the formation of energy and he may use it to again change to whatever state he wants. But that's not what happened. As matter is at last formed from us."

Green Energy continued, " As we changed the form, so the interaction also changed. The emotions also changed their forms for better communication with new species. I am also one of those positive energies, I exist in every living and non-living creature."

I asked, "That means you exist in humans too, But how?"

Green energy replied, "When matter was created, we thought that for proper balance of the Universe; there must be an intellectual being which is as intelligent as us, so beings which developed a full consciousness were human beings. We as Green Energies are the consciousness of your brain and positive emotions of your heart. Everything one desires to achieve and accomplish in this universe has its way through me. Positive emotions bring out happy and pleasant feelings and we are the energies which actually shape that positive attitude in the form of hormones. It helps you lead your life in an easy going manner and affects health in a beneficial way. It nurtures your working abilities and boosts the immune system. Developing and maintaining positivity isn't only about happy thoughts but it is the anticipation of good and its belief in that everything will work out favorably in the end."

I was stunned by the words of wisdom and the vibe that positive energy creates.
 I felt full of enthusiasm to know more and asked with great curiosity, "But what is your origin? How did you arise?"

Green energy replies, "As I previously said, I and other positive energies have existed since forever. Even though we transferred our form to matter, we still remain whether matter lives or dies. When a human dies, positive energy from his/her body gets transferred from one to another. I leave a soul after his death and venture into a new one upon his arrival in this universe. This universe, as a whole, is closed. However human bodies and all the other life forms existing on this planet are not closed- they're open systems. We exchange energies with our surroundings."

Green energy continues, " I cannot be traced perfectly but I can be sensed even in the toughest of times and in tons of little things that bring positive vibes or happiness in your life. There can be multiple ways people adopt me, it can be through helping others, developing an attitude of gratitude, taking little breaks, expressing and talking to our favorite person, laughing out loud, or doing something you like. I help out people to overcome tough phases of their life with a smile on their faces. I bring out a layer of optimism and a new way of looking towards the worries of life."

The teenager asks furiously, "Does that mean that you are our God? But my teacher didn't tell me that green energy is also a God to us.."

The energy makes the sound of laughter and gives a grinning look to the teenager. It said, " I'm perhaps the one that exists even in God. The whole universe is implanted by me. These figures of God are created by humans. They have idolized different people like Jesus, Shri Ram and Allah. But what makes them idolized is me. I existed in all of them and people were impressed by their lifestyle and the way they carried themselves. But each one of them always had truckloads of positive energies stored within them that made them do anything for the betterment of this world."

Green energy explains,"All these religion based differences are created by humans themselves. There's nothing like a separate God, religion and caste in the holy and divine books of religions like the Quran, Bible and Bhagavad-Gita. All of them strongly urge that every creature should be treated in this world with equal respect and everyone should stride towards a world embodied with harmony, peace and brotherhood. There should be no gender or caste based discrimination and everyone should live as if the world is one whole family."

Green energy continues,"In Fact every religion promotes one motto, that is- Hatred doesn't have any place in the world. Love is the only way to connect with the world. Love breaks all barriers including political, social, cultural, religious, racial and national. We are all the branches of one tree. The root is one. The world is our root; branches are the nations; and leaves are the people. Let us appreciate the fact that we all have originated from one place and we all belong to one family. Hence, the whole world is one family.

The bible insists on what happens when mankind is guided under the path of God, righteousness, faithfulness, mercy and love. It teaches us the etiquette of being a human with only a positive aura.

Green energy continues, "The Quran urges you to look into the blessings of your Lord and see if you could deny any of them. But if we see through this verse, it's not only a question. It's a pathway that leads you to the reflections of the favors that your Lord has granted you with. When you start speculating about the blessings you have in your life, this verse fills your heart with gratitude as it tells you that you have so much to be thankful for. It gives you a positive approach towards life."

"The Bhagavad-Gita says that there exists "arjuna" in every human being. At some point of time in our lives, we might be in a dilemma of making decisions and a confused state of mind can make us lose every battle of life. Hence, everything written in the holy book is like a mirror for the seeker as the text relieves its deeper meanings when the seeker develops a spiritual perspective. All the other Hindu Upanishads stress only one thing - "vasudhaiva kutumbakam" implying that the whole world is one family."

A question hits my mind. I asked the green energy, "Then what about all the wishes we ask from God? Who makes them come true or is it just for the sake of belief that they do come true?"

The green energy was very much impressed with the curiosity and avidity the teenager expressed. It seems as if he is very much interested in knowing how this world works. It said, "The wishes you ask from God are actually nothing but the greed of getting more than you can achieve. Thankfulness comes to a heart when he's been blessed with enough that others can't even possess. But humans in the recent Era have become more self-centered. They have millions of wishes which they seek from the Lord for their own benefit.

But these wishes give rise to a ray of hope within your own heart that one day your prayers will be answered. Such emotions keep rising up to that extent until you stop seeing the bad insinuations and feel like your wishes are coming true. The main objective behind this is increasing your own positivity and belief which becomes the solution to all your problems. You yourself are the source of making your troubles vanish. God is nothing but the visualization our ancestors created with the hope and optimism stored in their soul. The celebration of festivals also help to lighten hope in us, therefore everyone should try to celebrate all the festivals with full vigour, energy and enjoyment. "

I feel so astounded and thinks that he now has the knowledge of every religion existing in the world. He then asks the green energy, "But why am I able to see you!?"

The green energy replied, " There's a purpose behind everything that has ripened in life. You are the one chosen by the universe itself and that is the reason you've got to learn what impact I have on all of your lives. The main reason you get to know this is a mystery that time will untangle. Time will tell you the actual truth behind your unique selection from this whole vast universe."

Green energy continues, "When there came the existence of life forms in this universe, along with us, NEGATIVE ENERGY too, conquered it's existence. We, all positive energies, have thought that matter can't develop negative energy but we were wrong, matter and humans, all developed it. It arised due to the advancement of humans and their hunger for more.

It started taking our place when people became a rat and started chasing life. It all started when they started having increased lumps of hatred, jealousy, sadness, comparison, stress, rage amongst themselves. They had fears, of being missed out, of not being successful and many more but they forgot that like every coin has two sides, similar can be the approach towards life."

With the aim of having more, people develop a lot of negative energy within themselves and sometimes take steps that harm their own self as well as the others around them. They either do it unconsciously or consciously but they contribute to increasing the level of negativity in the atmosphere that directly affects everyone's life in some or the other way."

"But how is this energy bad for us?", I questioned.

The green ray took a deep sigh and said to the teenager,

"The world is meant to be going ahead with harmony and peace.
But the negative emotions have put all of it to a cease.
People are becoming self centered and emotionless,
Is making it grow into a big success.
Engrossed into groans and griefs of life,
Makes positive energy more difficult to survive."

I was awestruck when I heard the trembling effects of this energy. I suggested "then why don't you remove people who are so bad and who have such energy in themselves?"

The green energy gave him a cold look. It said, "you also have this kind of energy stored in you but your positive energy overcomes it. The death of loved ones can make you feel tons of negative emotions and lead you to a path that is undesired. In your case, when you lost Mary, you developed immense hate towards (boy) and the group one. Your heart sank in guilt, sorrow and a new fear of losing the ones you love. All these fears make you tremble."

"When you lose someone, you should rather see the bright side in their death. One should see that if one person goes, then it gives rise to another, as energy from that dead person transfers to a newborn baby. Death of someone should be cherished because at that moment, you should recollect all the great times you've spent together with that person and be grateful for having them in your life. Looking for the bright side even in the darkest of times - Hope - is what means to be having positive energy. Being happy and satisfied in your life increases positive energy in your body."

"Moreover, it's not the people who are bad, it's the circumstances that make them bad. No person is bad but the troubles life has thrown on them makes them overlook the positivity in the world and develop feelings of anger, jealousy and hatred. Everyone faces such kinds of things once in his life but the one who knows how to overcome it and be a good human being no matter what, is considered as a true image of a human being I created."

A gust of self realization surrounds the teenager.

I thought about how the unexpected death of Mary developed these emotions inside me. I had never, before the death of Mary, thought bad about anyone. I became aware how important it was to stop the War that was going on. All the people had developed loath, hatred and jealousy among themselves which led to this attempt of ultimate destruction of the world.

<div align="center">~~~~~~~~</div>

Again there was a huge thunder of light. I could barely see what was happening around me. I was shaking and my organs were vibrating. I suddenly felt a strong jerk and my body felt as if something was getting into it with immense pressure. I felt like I was being injected with something that is the strongest. My nerves were twitching as if high volts of electricity had passed through them. I almost lost my senses. I couldn't feel my organs and all I could sense was the tugging of a strong substance inside me. I was all confused when a voice suddenly raised within me.

It mumbled, " I am the same energy that was talking to you in the form of a flash. But as I told you the purpose of your lone existence, I've entered inside you."

I was astounded. I was filled with confusion and questions about the sudden arrival of green energy in his body. I asked the green energy, "What are you doing inside me? What do you want me to do?"

Green Energy speaking inside my mind, "Now that I've entered into you, I want you to convey to everyone what is the purpose of their existence. Everyone has developed a negative aspect of chasing things that people don't even desire but want to acquire just because others possess it and the world has made it an example of perfection. Humans have to rise above all sorts of negative emotions flooding inside a human heart such as anger, envy, hatred and jealousy. We have to end this war but that is not by killing the wrong ones but making them right and noble. This war is going to be different from history as no-one will be killed, everyone will end the war mutually by sorting their differences and developing compassion for each other. Therefore, we will time travel to a time before the start of war and all the deaths that occurred and you have to convince everyone to stop this war and understand their purpose of life."

"World has to be filled up with chunks of elements like happiness, motivation, peace and love for everyone around you to actually make this world a better place to live in. Now Leo, it is your mission. Are you ready to take it?"

I said, "Yes."

~~~~~~~

After this, everything becomes silent. The echoing voice of the green energy is now as silent as a grave. I was also quiet.

I couldn't see anything in my surroundings. All the stars have disappeared and the sky was empty. But there was something that was still shining. My heart was in a jumbled state. Millions of thoughts rushed inside me. To calm the whirling tornado beneath my cold and immovable body, I closed my eyes for a while. I was numb. A different feeling tickled my soul. I never felt this way before.

After a few moments when I gradually opened my eyes, I found myself in a whole different scenario. I wasn't amidst the stars now. It seemed like a known place. A place I had been living in since a considerate time. When
~~~~~~~

I looked around myself, I saw things imprinted on my mind like I saw them earlier.

And yes, I finally figured it out.

It was the time-machine that took me away from my home. The same time-machine where I found new friends. Everything inside it looked the way it was earlier. There was a rush of robotic equipment all over the place. Every little thing is retained to its original place. The main boisterous mouth, the tables and chairs aligned on the left side of the entrance and a huge robot placed centrally inside it. Everyone was in their places and so was the love of my life, my Mary.

She was working in her room with her weapons and IOT gadgets. She looked so composed and focused while she was looking at the screen. My heart skipped a beat when I saw her. Tears arose in my eyes as I recalled her death and asked myself, "Why I doubted her, fought with her during her last days". I really felt extremely guilty about it.

I asked the Green energy inside me, "At what point of time are we?"

It said to me, "We are at that point of time, where you doubted Mary of loving Aktio and fooling you. Today's evening is the time when she will discover Sahil taking the briefcase to Thinker and will ultimately die in the evening. Today you were out of time-machine, somewhere with Jessie as you felt hurt. Therefore I brought you in this time, so that you get a second chance to spend more time with Mary and express your feelings to her."

I said, with watery eyes, "Thanks a lot for this favour."

I happily went to her, and placed my hands on her gentle eyes to surprise her. She immediately raised her hands and put them on mine. I knew that she could never fail to guess who it was.

She squeaked, "Finally! You are here. So, what were you talking about me and Akito? Why have you deserted me for three days. I was feeling so alone without you" she said, with a few tears in her eyes and a gloomy expression.

I pulled my hands off and looked her in the eyes. I said, "Look marina, I am genuinely sorry for my behavior. I promise I will never do that again." I wanted to not waste a single minute in that discussion.

Her face was blank. I couldn't really guess what she was thinking. Her lips were locked and her eyes seemed as if it was a deep down forest that had a long way to go. After a few seconds she spoke.

She said, " Nice Leo. I am happy to see you back with full spirit."

I smiled seeing her smile. But deep down I knew this wouldn't last for long. She is going to be drifted apart from me forever. Therefore I want to create these last hours of her's as the happiest moments of her life.

So I asked her whether she would like to go on a coffee date with me. At first she hesitated as there was a lot of worl to do. But I was desperate to make her feel like the happiest person. She said that she would love it if they went for it some other day. How should I tell her that this is last day....

I told her, "Mary, life is too short to put things on tomorrow. It's always these little jocund memories that are captured in our hearts and remain embedded in our memory lane until we dissolve into ashes. Everything is unpredictable. What if one of us gets trapped in some trouble we can never come out of!? What if we never get to see each other again!?" My eyes again got watery.

She gave me a confused look, as since she knew me, I never talked like this.

I was feeling extremely low and I turned my face sidewards for a second to hide my sadness that flooded on my flushed face. She grabbed my shoulder and insisted on sparing some time to let her get ready. I told her, "what things or tools could ever make a divine goddess of beauty look more beautiful!! She was already a quintessence of magic." She blushed and went off to get ready.

While I was standing there I talked to Sahil, Akito and others. I am really so gleeful to see them back in life. I just suddenly replied that I love you all. They passed me a smile and continued chit-chatting about the bomb.

While my eyes were focused on the hallway, she came, wearing a milky white robe embroidered with pearls and silver threads. It wasn't an IOT dress, just a normal one. She was looking stunning. My heart went in awe when I saw her. The ivory choker on her neck was complimenting her dress. Her golden hairs were beautifully braided and tied with a ribbon. She walked a few meters and came to me. I took her hand and kissed her as if she was the most beautiful girl I have ever seen. Her cheeks become rosy and a wave of shyness rose over her. We went for the date hand in hand looking towards each other.

As I knew I would lose her to death a few hours later, I decided to tell her what I felt for her. She was secretly glaring at me. I held her hand. It wasn't a casual hold. I held it so tightly like I never wanted to let go. She didn't say anything. Then she turned and looked into my eyes. It was a deep stare. Neither of us said a word but if felt like our eyes confessed every little ounce of what we felt. How ironic it was that the silence spoke so loud and clear. I could feel the affection towards me in her eyes. It felt like her eyes were an ocean of emotions and I was sinking in.

My eyes became gloomy and red again to think of a life without her after a few hours. Tears rolled down my cheeks and my lips trembled to even speak a word. I knew the reality but I can't tell her anything as Green energy said that it will change the future. My heart was clutching and sinking. I didn't want to lose her. No, not at any cost could I lose the one whom I love the most in the world. A voice inside me wanted to scream and cry loudly but was getting suppressed by my silence. I couldn't do anything but just cried my heart out. After we sat on a table in the garden to order some food, I started crying immensely.

Mary got startled to see me crying. She was panicking and constantly asking me what happened. I couldn't utter a word. How should I tell her that I know everything but I still cannot save her.

That's when everything just paused and a green emit of light arised in me. It was the green energy. Whilst I was crying and sobbing in pain, it uttered, "Teenager, handle yourself. Everything in this universe is planned. You have to control your emotions and come out as a strong person."

I replied, "how do you expect me to be strong in such a situation? I am about to lose the love of my life, a pure soul I never met before. You are such a strong energy. Please do some magic. Please save her. I beg you. I can't imagine how it would be living without her. She adds so much charm and happiness to my life. Please green energy, don't let her die. I would die without her!"

"Think about humanity teenager!" The energy said. The only thing you are concerned with is the death of your loved one. You cannot change the past just to save one life. If you do so, the whole future gets changed. Widen your view for humanity, if I prevent her from dying, you won't be able to get the voice password of the briefcase and you won't be able to blast the Universe and then you won't find me. This way it will lead to billions of other deaths."

The energy consoled me. It gave me a broader view to look upon. I chanted my God's name. "For those who believe in him could cross any obstacle that obstructs their path."

I felt a little calm. There was a touch on my shoulder. It was Mary's hand. Everything became normal again. Mary was looking at my gloomy face and she wiped my tears with her silk handkerchief.

She still kept asking me why I was crying. I didn't say anything. I just held her hand and tenderly kissed her forehead.

In that moment, I felt nothing but just so full of love for her. It was a deep feeling. Just as a wanderer finally found a shelter. Just as a thirsty seeker found a bowl of water. Just as the heated deserts finally witnessed the first rain showers. Just as a musician finally found the perfect lyrics for his song. It felt like it was only the two of us and a sheath of pure love and comfort that separated us from everyone else. I was with her, sitting hand in hand, not an inch apart. Her existence was like adjective and I was the noun, she defines me. She was the imprint and I was the nostalgia. She was the resonance and I was her emotional string. Her presence does to me what moon does to romance, what a fairy does to a tale and what Tagore did to the poems. She adds so tinch of completeness to me.
Our eye contact was intact. It seemed as if her eyes were the Crystal Ball of magic through which we were trying to understand our own self and foresee the true reason of our being. My lips slowly travelled down her smooth skin towards her bubbly cheeks. I gave delicate kisses on both of her cheeks as well. She was also lost in the tranquilness of time. My lips slowly travelled towards hers. There was a softness like petals. Our tongues met. Lips were locked. Our souls mingled. It was a feeling beyond words.

After a few seconds of immeasurable love, she stopped and hugged me tightly. I didn't refuse and took her in my arms. She stuck to me like glue. I wrapped her.

A bubble of feelings rushed in my heart. I thought about how beautiful the feeling of loving and being loved back was.

"The rushing gush of adrenaline,
And the tingles of the first crush running over your skin.
It feels like a whole new adventure of life,
When someone's presence makes you grin.
It hits differently when for the very first time,

You feel love running in your veins.
For someone who seems just perfect to you,
The one that sets you free from all your pains."

In that moment I realized, that the human body takes nine months to be born but it takes only one instant to connect ourselves, emotionally, mentally, physically, I'd say in every possible way.

But the eagle of the anticipated truth was soon to perch on its prey. I knew there was a right time for everything and I was grateful enough to get this moment with Mary. I had to close this chapter as it was the time for another one to unfold. I bid Mary farewell and said we'll meet soon but I know that we will not be able to meet again. She went to her work and I closed my eyes and swallowed lumps of pain as I knew the moment I opened it, she would be gone, gone forever.

I again time-travelled with Green energy. When I blinked back nothing was the same. I found myself in Thinker's spaceship and Green energy whispered in my ears, "You're invisible to everyone." At a certain distance, I saw Mary.

I started running towards her desperately. As I was running, Thinker shot electricity on her.

Oh my God! She is dying....

I couldn't even think of the word in my head. The feeling I felt next is one that I can describe as equivalent to getting hit in the stomach with a sledgehammer. I stumbled backward and fell. I started weeping seeing her falling to the ground at the turtle's pace. I immediately got up and handled her body as it fell to the ground. I wasn't visible to anyone but I think Mary would have felt my presence. I could see her soul volatilized from her body to the atmosphere bit by bit. It was killing me on the inner edge. I wanted to shout and let her know that I love her! I loved her so much that no one could ever do it! She was my everything. Within a millisecond, I lost everything. My heart was shattered, my hands were caressing her golden hairs covered in blood, my lips trembled and I gave an intense kiss on her forehead knowing it was the last kiss, the final goodbye kiss!

I was heaved with sadness as I couldn't do anything even after being there. I couldn't just witness her death in front of my eyes and shout, " Oh, green energy! Help me. I can't see her dying in front of me. I want to save her. I want to wrap her in my arms and protect her. She is my everything."

After a long interval, the energy said something. It exclaimed, "This cannot happen Leo. This situation is a segment of past. I said you that you can't change the past even if you wish to. Changing it will have drastically effects both on your present as well as your future.

What your eyes are seeing is the death of your loved one but what I am observing is how stopping this death will lead to deaths of many others.

I said in a melancholic tone, "But how should I let her die?"

Green energy said, "Death is important in the world as it teaches us to value the life we have, to value our time. It puts things into perspective. Death brings you to life. Death, the awareness of Death, to the point of no return, wakes you up to the reality of your oneness in existence. Therefore, Death is what makes our life precious and we can't avoid it or reject it."

"You cannot die, if you don't believe in Death,
because you've never feared it.
But you die the moment you are scared of it,
Because that binds you from living your life to the fullest."

Furious teenager screamed, "But why!? Why can't I live a little longer with her? I want to hold her once again, I want to love her forever till the old-age. Why can't we live with each other till our old-age and then we may die happily?"

Green energy replies with a sigh of grief, "You should learn to embrace the time you spent together, dear. Love just seems to be a four letter word, but it is actually deeper, taller and wider than skyscrapers, monuments and the oceans. It is an immortal and eternal feeling. It is not just about the physical presence but the intermingling of emotional and soulful connections between the two souls.

You don't know how much someone's lifespan is going to be before they actually die. Is she/he will be with me forever or I have to survive without her/him. These remain unanswered until a wave of reality hits the gentle winds of love. Therefore try to be with your loved one for as much time as possible. No-one knows which may be your last kiss. Even if you have loved someone with all your heart then it doesn't matter whether she is dead or alive, the bond ,the chemistry between you always remains eternal. You can feel them around you when you need them the most, they will act as a guardian, as an angel to you when you are in times of distress, for love is the feeling of tranquilness in this chaotic world. Love gives you a whole new reason to live life, a life with or without your loved one, a life that is truly lived for her."

"But why does love give us so much pain?" I asked

The green energy said,
"A true love is seen as one where you feel the happiness, pain, grieving and every other emotion of your loved one as yours. Happiness and pain is all a part of a unit called love and this is what truly constitutes the meaning of love."

"I wish I didn't have doubted and ignored her. That way I would have spent a little more time with her." I was frustrated and in deep regret about his deed.

Green energy continues, "That is why I say Leo, life is so unpredictable and unknown. It may take drastic changes in a little moment. No one knows how much they are going to live. We often indulge into fights that lead to misunderstandings between the strongest of our bonds. We let them continue assuming that one day misunderstanding will automatically get vanished. But we shouldn't wait for such a time because no one has seen the future, everyone should try to solve the misunderstandings at present by keeping their ego aside, which will help us to spend more time with our loved ones. When your loved one die, what remains is regret, regret of not resolving the bitterness of our relationships and not telling the one how much you love them. The time you spent quarreling with them, instead could have been the moments you loved them a little more."

"How comforting it was when she was around me . I miss her presence. Can you do anything about this feeling?" I asked.

Energy replied, " As I live in every bit of a human, therefore when someone dies, they also release me (positive energy) from themselves. But as I said, I never vanished, I get transferred to a newborn but a part of me gets embedded in every other human that is connected with the dying soul. My part reminds everyone that their loved one is still with them. This is the real essence of love, therefore you never feel separated from your loved one."

I now cleaned my eyes and took a deep breath and asked," I lost the one whom I love the most. I don't think there's anything you and I can do about it! But what do I do now?"

Green energy continued," Leo, You have to accept Mary's death and also realize that a love like yours is also a segment of the thread of pure love that is everlasting. Mariana's death was a part of the sacrifice she made for the love she had, and will always have, for you and this would set an example for the rest of the generations to come. Her sacrifice will be cherished. And you don't have to let her efforts get into vain, her selfless sacrifice should get justice. The justice that only you can bring to her.

You have to complete the mission for which I brought you here. You have to preach to the world about the importance of love and affection and its effect on humanity as a whole. You have to let the world know that a life lived for love, with love is really a life worth living. You have to stop the world War and teach people a lesson that will bring about unity and harmony in this world that is walking on a path of cruelty."

CHAPTER 9

THE NEW WORLD

We come back to the day when the Thinker army is attacking us. At this point, no one has died. I was, at this point in the basecamp of the Urja group at Saturn's moon.

I asked Green Energy, "What about my past self? If I'm in this time, and if we stop the war, what will happen to him?"

Green energy responded, "He will disappear as when future will change, he will lose his creation as time-space will get affected. So, in simple words, you will only be there left and no other Leo."

Green energy said that," Now, I'm connecting everyone with your conscience. Therefore everyone will be able to hear what you are saying..."

Suddenly the world became connected. Each and every human mind got linked to Leo's mind. The whole world was binded together not through the channel of words but through the channel of emotions and thoughts.

Now Leo thought, and everyone heard him-

"The world altogether is like a global village. We all are children of the same father. Everyone is born with an Individual motive in their life. But the ultimate achievement of a human is considered when he finds out his purpose of life."

Everyone got shocked when they started hearing voices in their ears. Thinker and his group were also hearing this.

I continued, "I have connected all of you to my mind. I want everyone of you to understand that we should end the war. When the creator made this world, he put on his best elements like love, compassion, empathy, brotherhood, togetherness and above all humanity. Each and everyone existing in this world are bonded together by humanity. The race of chasing excellence in advanced technologies and perfections has made us blind and unknown to the philosophies of the world. They have forgotten the core reason for their existence. Our purpose of life is to achieve happiness and not Success."

Thinker, with his highly intellectual mind and thinking IOT chair, manages to question Leo in his thoughts. He asks:
"Who are you? Why do you want to change our attitude to life? Even what is happiness according to you, just enjoying with money?"

I took a pause. I cleared my mind of any thoughts that rumbled inside, then I gently closed the shutter of my eyes and took a deep breath. Everything was as silent as a grave.

I took a few more deep breaths and tried to feel everything that existed around me. I could hear the melodious chirping of the birds that occupied the vast and widespread conifers. I could hear the jingling sound of swinging leaves as they danced upon the tunes played by the gentle moving breeze.

The voice of tender water hitting the lap of shores. The swaying and serene winds that touch the face from the outside but tingles the soul up till the verge. Witnessing the flowers bloom during the spring season. Seeing the plants nurturing and dancing during the evening. Finding happiness in the drops of first rain that feeds the hunger of dry earth.

I finally spoke, "No... money is not happiness. Happiness is spending time taking a walk in nature and witnessing the tranquility that resides in its lap. Happiness is smelling the sweet fragrance of flowers in the garden or witnessing the bright and playful colors displayed by nature. Happiness is spending time with your loved ones and giggling with them throughout the day, having long talks with your favorite person and realizing you have got someone's back to rely onto. Happiness is the feeling which you feel when you genuinely help someone. Everything that refreshes your mind and fills up your heart with cheerfulness and joy is happiness. Happiness exists in every little thing that we do in our daily life, it just needs to be recognized."

"But why do we need such emotions? Our life's purpose is to develop and take this world to a whole new level of advancement. Emotions make us weak, therefore we should not think of happiness but we should work for development." Dashed thinker.

I said, "The curtain of forwardness and excellence has made this world blind.
The feeling of negativeness has made their emotions grind.
They've forgotten the worldly treasures the creator has blessed them with,
Running behind success gives happiness is purely a myth."

I continued in the same poetic form to make everyone understand this point,

"The sufferings we face in life,
Transforms us into something we are not.
To our happy emotions and thoughts,
It brings it to a halt.
But we must not forget that bad clouds get away,
And there is always a new day full of sunshine.
With the loudest cheer of togetherness, peace and harmony,
Living up with happiness and contentment is as satisfactory as worshipping in a shrine."

I continued, "I mean to say that of course advancement and progress is necessary for our world and for new generations but why should we live a life where there is no happiness for us. We exist for a purpose and that is to contribute to the world but also make our existence a memorable one so that when we are about to die, we can say, 'it was a beautiful and jocund life. Thank God for giving it'."

Thinker again makes a statement. "Ok. It can be the case, but why are you explaining about happiness now. We are in a state of War."

I said patiently, "Therefore Dear Thinker, I want everyone of you to end this piece of destruction which does nothing but take away your happiness from you."

Thinker got amazed as I denoted him as 'Dear', no one ever spoke so friendly to him ever.

Thinker said, "We are fighting for the purpose of happiness. After war, we will create a new Universe where everyone will work for advancement, and everyone will be happy. So let us make our Universe, why are you coming in our path."

I explained in a sweet note, "Happiness is therefore a very complex emotion and can't be easily understood. But we feel happiness not just by working hard or by making life easier or by achieving success. We feel real happiness when we are compassionate to others. When we connect to others, when we try to reduce their hardships without demanding anything in return, at that point we feel the most pure form of happiness. The more we communicate with people, the more we connect to this world. So, real happiness lies not in materialistic achievements but in emotional bonds. Just remember the happiness you felt when you helped someone. Did it give you a serene feeling when you witness the smile of a person whom you've helped? The innocence and gratefulness in their smile makes you feel like thousands of sunflowers have blossomed and are smiling back at you. The fresh green grass is moving to and fro and patting your back saying that you've done a good job. This is happiness and this is our purpose of life to be emotionally connected with others and live with harmony and compassion.

"But how can one's happiness be in someone else? Happiness is a feeling bound to your soul. How can it be extracted from others? Listening to others' problems can make you more stressed. Then how is it a source of happiness?" Added thinker.

I answered in a happy tone, "It may seem that by knowing people's problems, we are entering into their mess but the more you get to know people, the more you know how sorted your life is. When we understand the difficulties others face in their lives, we start being grateful for our lives and even start fighting our problems. Once you see the people indirectly connected to you, your watchman, who has to work all night and day and get so little paid. Child laborers, who are not able to receive education, even if they want, and have to work from such a tinder age to live. Poor people, who don't get opportunities to show their talents. People of the Middle East who face so many difficulties including hunger, unemployment, lack of freedom, suppression, etc. Now again think if your life is better than theirs or not. Even we as humans are genetically made in this way. When we help others, happiness delivering hormones activate in our body which helps us to feel this pleasant feeling."

"Yes, you make a good point. But one cannot always stay happy in his life. What about the times when he feels extremely low and confused!? How will he find happiness in such a state of mind?" Thinker asked, in a tone as if now he is changing his thoughts.

I explained, "When we are on the happy page of our chapter, we never ought to think what the sad phase might be like. This is why we are never ready to face the challenges. Rather, one can develop himself in a way that when the problems encounter him and encircle him in the web of developing negative emotions, he should be strong enough to face them and perceive good in everything."

I continued," When trust is shattered, when hopes are dashed, when a loved one leaves you, before doing anything, just pause your life and rest a moment. It is obvious that in these circumstances no one can stay happy, but during this time, take a break from the emotions that stress you."

"If you are unable to change a bad situation, even after many attempts, you should change how you look at the situation. Understand that nothing is intrinsically good or bad. Compare your situation with someone's that is worse. Now yours won't seem so bad after all."

Thinker asked patiently as if now he is believing in the power of emotions, "But everyone has to die one or the other day, so is it not right to chase success and fame that makes the world recognize you, as no one will remember you for being happy."

I was suddenly filled with mixed thoughts. I got flashbacks of the time I witnessed Mariana's death in front of my eyes. It was so painful and heart wrenching to watch the love of my life falling apart from the chapters of my life ahead. But then I remember the words of wisdom the green energy imparted to me that my love won't be sacrificed but would rather be cherished for ages and remain immortal if I succeed in changing the world, even a little bit.

After thinking of Mary, I continued, "Yes Thinker, the world remembers you for your contributions therefore as I said that we will feel real happiness when we connect to others by helping them. So, by doing something beneficial for society or helping people, we get happiness as well as recognition. Even if we don't get recognition for our good deeds, at least the people, whom we help, will remember us forever and they will be there for us if we need any help. Therefore you should be content with limited recognition also. Look for love not for fame. Being content relaxes our endless striving and welcomes serenity. It helps us to make peace with our past deeds."

Thinker sweetly asked, "But what if we don't make a big contribution to the world. What if we are ourselves in problems, then how can we help others." From his voice it seemed like he was developing compassion in his heart.

I answered, "How often do we express our feelings to someone we love? Maybe everyday, every week or every month? But did we ever realise how often we looked in the mirror, and praise yourself and said, 'you are doing the best you can. You are courageous enough to give it a try. You are worth it. I love you'. Self-love is one of the key components that lead to contentment and inner peace. Accepting yourself the way you are is the greatest realisation that can dawn you. Peace comes from within. And that within has to be pure and free of negative emotions about yourself and the world to be able to achieve inner peace. When you love yourself, when one is happy with his life, then only he/she can make others happy and love others."

The thinker is dawned by the light of reality. He feels a gamut of emotions that are tangled on his mind just like millions of cables. He is confused and whenever he is not able to answer mysteries of life, he sees the face of someone who has died long ago, someone who brought him into this world, someone who patted his head but also exposed him to the harsh and bitter realities of life, someone who gave him preaching like a nun, scolding like a teacher, advice like a friend, showed him way like a guide and of course, the love that nobody can give, the love of a mother.

He witnessed her presence around him whenever life encircled him with problems. She was a lady with a peaceful aura and a happy face. There was always a layer of calmness over her pretty, bright face.

I am able to feel those memories of Thinker. I can feel that:-

Right from the beginning of his life, the only thing Thinker faced was struggles. His father passed away during his childhood and the only meaning of family to him was his beloved mother. She had always been enough. She was a social worker who tried to find happiness in others. She believed that being happy is the ultimate achievement of a human in his entire life.

Thinker always used to listen to her philosophies with great concentration and interest. It felt as if after God, her mother knew it all.

But life is harsh. Her mother faced a lot of struggles in her early life that made them live a miserable life. They never had enough resources to lead a luxurious life. His mother worked hard to let him have a life of his dreams. She struggled each day with a positive attitude for Thinker.

Then finally, the eagle of life perched its prey. She died when the thinker was young. He was shattered and his heart was thumped. Everyone around him told him that his mother died because of her social works that disturbed a few groups of people who had a traditional religious mindset. They told him that she was a cretin who believed happiness is important.

Thinker was confused, he didn't know what to believe. There was a little corner in his heart that wanted to believe what his mother always told him. He somehow altered his shattered pieces and followed the path opposite to what his mother guided him to.

Heading into the teenage years, Thinker fell in love with a beautiful young woman with an attractive smile and a charming face. She was the most famous girl in high school. Everyone was literally in awe with her beauty.

By luck or by chance, Thinker got lucky and they both developed feelings for each other. It was a good phase of his life. It seemed as if thousands of flowers bloomed during the spring and just like new leaves emerged on the branches, his heart was blossoming with feelings of love and affection.

They had a great time together and had a lot in common. They felt happy whenever they were around each other. It was a feeling like no other.

But this happiness was only short lived. She cheated on him. Only thing he was left with was bleeding memories of heartbreak and suffering. His scratches of the past were re-hurting. This added salt to his burns. The past laid unburied in front of him.

He still managed to keep himself calm and thought of the words his mother imparted him. But once the glass gets broken, it cannot be mended again. His heart started feeling negative emotions like sadness, grief and pains.

This took a sharp edge when his very own best friend, the one whom he trusted the most, betrayed him and broke his trust. His heart was filled with jealousy, anger and hatred. The corner of wisdom that his mother engraved within his heart started to fade away. Even when he started working as an intellect, he tried many things to help people but in each effort, he got resistance from people and society because of which he finally developed this kind of attitude as prevailing in him today.

Like others, he also started believing that there is nothing like happiness and contentment. He started believing that emotionally connecting with others led to a miserable life full of sufferings. The only way by which you can have a luxury life is success. Technical advancements and self-centered nature can only drive you to a successful path.

But now as I became a part of his known world, his mindset is beginning to change again.

He is awestruck by the kind words of mine and relates to the situations he marked where one attains happiness.

He recalls his past when his mother was alive, and he used to help her in NGO work like delivering clothes to the poor and widow women living there. The widest smile he could ever witness was on their face when he handed it over to them. It filled his heart with pride and satisfaction to help others. Their grateful and kind words made him feel privileged to be among the ones who can make this world a better place to live in.

He had several times, during his childhood, fed the poor and needy when he didn't want to eat. Their content faces fed his not-so-hungry stomach with pleasure. During his high school days, he had a good bunch of friends and he was always up whenever they needed some help. Even Though he wasn't rich enough, he did his bit to help his best friend during his suffering times.

Thinker finally says, "I'm now surrounded by a gust of awareness. I think that my past has made me so shattered, and stone hearted. I had become like the people who had hurt me. I got turned down like the ones who betrayed me and broke my heart. World doesn't need people like me."

This is heard by Leo as well as all others.

Thinker continues, "If I become like them, what is the difference between me and them. I understood that all my plans were wrong as if everyone became so self-centered for their own happiness, no one will actually be able to attain it.. I realised that I have been chasing the wrong path. We don't need a new Universe, we don't just need modernization but with it we need love and compassion in our society and I'm ready to make a World like it along with everyone."

Everyone responded the same, "We are with you. We'll make a World where Love is more important than development."

Thinker finally asks with a childish curiosity, "Thanks for being our **Saviour** and teaching us the purpose of our lives. Can you just say, what and who are you?"

I replied, "I'm the God who lives inside all of you."

The connection with Leo's mind and others finally breaks. Thinker gets live and says to everyone," I apologise for all my wrong deeds which devoid love. I am here ready to end war and I'll develop new strategies to lead the World. In just a few months, we will change our World, we will change the way we live life, we will increase the happiness of our lives. I apologise to the Urja team's Commander for all the difficulties they faced because of me. I'm going to meet him this week to discuss the New World. I regret thinking of Mariana's demise and will make her sacrifice, a day of national honour. Now we will change our world to a much better one and we will safely keep Dr. Vikram's briefcase without disturbing it until we are ready to use it in a positive way. Thank You everyone."

Green energy was still inside me. I went to meet all my friends and we are extremely happy to hear that War is finally over.

I can describe that feeling as:

"Just like after a stormy night comes a day of bright sunbeams
Similarly happiness will emerge no matter how hidden it may seem.
Life is too little to be entrapped into negative feelings,
Rather be with people who act as healings.
Live a life full of Love and contentment,
War has ended and a new life is commencing."

~~~~~~

As Thinker said, within a few months, the world got completely changed. Thinker became a generous, empathetic leader and made Commander as incharge of World Army. People who were sent to Dreamscape - The
~~~~~~

Program of Dreams - were brought back to life. Family unions happened. Sahil, Jessie and Akito met their parents and siblings who were sent to Dreamscape for being not intelligent and less talented. But Thinker has now made a World, not one which just focuses on development but one which focuses on human values, love and happiness. Not just The Thinker, everyone understood that their purpose in life is to bring happiness and love into the world along with development.

All the harmful technologies were dismantled. A.I. programs still existed but in sectors where they help humans instead of eliminating them. For example: A.I. programs remain in Medical sector to help doctors and prevent lives but A.I. programs of war were destroyed. Legal A.I. programs were there which settled legal disputes in seconds but were not put much in use as people neglected legal disputes, instead they solved their disputes with affection and empathy. Everyone was happy as everyone is concerned for the happiness of others. This is what I preached to everyone with the help of Green Energy: "World can be happy only when people love each other and work in a selfless manner for the benefit of society, others and themselves.

As less intelligent people - From Dreamscape - were also back in World, Thinker thought of ways to generate employment for them, so as to make World living place for everyone. The Thinker started embracing the inner talents of people and therefore many new creative fields emerged which benefited the society and employed a large number of people, again I can't say those to keep the future enact. Apart from creative fields, people were employed on other planets and habitation started taking place there. The new opportunities on other planets were: Businesses over there, space exploration, space architecture, lazer mining, making IOT gadgets there, space agriculture, etc. These fields employed almost everyone living and no-one remained unemployed. Even A.I. was used in the above jobs to make human work easier, so that humans can focus on more challenging jobs.

Apart from work, everyone have enough time to spend time with their families and friends. Corporates themselves motivated every employee to maintain healthy relationships and have a good social life. Even the intrinsic difference in the world narrowed down as there were few rich and most people earned enough to live a good life. No one is more concerned about money, everyone understands that their priority is Happiness and nothing else. Everyone started helping society and others in all the possible ways. Everyone got so connected to others of different origin, sex, colour, as if they all belong to just one family. Rich tried to help people with less income in every possible way, and not just they help, many Rich people had their best friends who were earning less, and those somewhat poor friends were always ready to help their rich buddies whenever required. This symbolised that money doesn't define true friendship. Thus, everyone attained state of Nirvana and finally love prevailed everywhere. The World became a Utopian state, just like what Dr. Vikram.... Dr. Vikram Bhatt wanted.

I enjoyed these last few months with my friends, commander and with memories of my love, Mary. I was no more sad whenever I got glimpses of her, instead I felt her presence which made me happy. I say to her in my mind that I made her dream come true, as I stopped the War without any deaths.. Finally as I got all my memories back, I have to go back in time, to live my life there. Commander told me that when I reach my time, I will forget all the memories of the future and they will forget everything about me, because of time-space change. Finally, my friends come to drop me back near my home in Manali in 2021, at the same time-machine. We finally hugged each other and cried. I said, "I will miss you Sahil, just keep making everyone laugh. Akito, sorry for everything, I hope you get a very good future. Jessie, I wish the same for you. And at last thankyou Commander for everything you did to me." Everyone got emotional and finally they left me in the same forest and went away.

I heard again the voice of Green Energy, "Well Done Leo, you accomplished your mission. Now just go to sleep. When you wake up, you won't remember anything about the future." Suddenly I got unconscious and fell down on the snow.

I heard a voice, "Hey, where were you. You disappeared for almost 15 mins. Why did you run away in the forest."

I opened my eyes and saw that the voice was of Nitya. I am confused and can't recall anything. I said, "What happened, and what is my name?"

Suddenly a sweet voice came behind Mary. She said, "You forgot you are Vicky."

I uttered, "What.... Please say my full name and by the way, who are you?"

She said, "Oh God! How can you forget it? I'm your best friend Mariana and you call me Mary, and you are Vikram Bhatt."

~~~~~~~

Green energy to readers:
"Hello dear readers, as you all may have guessed that **Dr. Vikram is none other than Leo**. It seems strange as the time-travel is really very strange. Even as Leo loved Mary in the 24th century, he in his time also fell in love, and got married to the same person and of the same qualities: Mary. This shows that true love mingles always and is not restricted by space and time. Leo only ends up discovering the anti-matter wave and makes the Briefcase, and the world knows him as Dr. Vikram. But as I say, that when you travel time, the future changes. This time also future may change as Leo, young Vikram, actually researched the anti-matter wave and made his Briefcase because he was somewhat pessimistic of the future as he thought that if War happened, his Briefcase will help to save the world or create a new one. But if young Vikram becomes more positive about the future then the anti-matter wouldn't be founded and Future War would never happen. So, if Leo says that he thinks that 'future is beautiful' then war will never happen but if he says that 'future is dark' then the future you
~~~~~~~

all saw, the same will happen when you will come in the 24th century. Let's see what he says."

~~~~~~

I, young Vikram, said, "Yeah now I remember everything."

Mary asks, "So you were sad for the future. Are you still sad about it or have you changed your opinion?"

I replied, " Yes. Future is filled with mysteries, the World may witness many changes, new technologies will develop, people will change and society will transform. So, finally I think the FUTURE IS......................"

~~~~~~ **THE END** ~~~~~~